EVIL INJUSTICE

Evil Injustice

Linda Lonsdorf

To order additional copies of this book, contact:
Xlibris Corporation
1-888-795-4274
www.Xlibris.com
Orders@Xlibris.com
107147

DEDICATION

To my wonderful, supportive, kind and gentle husband, Kevin Lonsdorf, who is my rock. He is a man of integrity and compassion, and he walks the walk everyday. He is my Doug Conrad.

ACKNOWLEDGEMENTS

Thanks goes to retired Captain James Yocum of the Akron Police Department for his help with police procedures. Thanks also goes to Mike Kakoules, a former police officer, public safety teacher, and detective for helping me with investigative techniques. A special thanks also goes to Summit County Prosecutor Mary Ann Kovach for verifying prosecution procedures used in the book. I also want to thank Dr. W.K. Lonsdorf, my husband, for his help on the medical issues along with Firemedic Keith Geiger from the City of Green Fire Department for his help with emergency procedures.

A very special thanks goes to Tom Secrest, a former high school friend and classmate for designing my book cover, and to Andy Pfaff, owner of Lyons Photography, for taking my photograph for the back cover.

PROLOGUE

Doug Conrad, a private investigator, and his family had become targets of a convicted killer, Quinton Reed, whom Conrad had been responsible for sending away to prison for fifteen years.

Doug's wife, Cynthia, had been abducted and then five days later murdered by Reed. Reed cajoled his youngest son, Kevin, into kidnapping Conrad's daughter, Taylor, a sophomore at Kent State University. Reed's plan to destroy Conrad's entire family failed when Reed broke into Mitch Neubauers' home, Conrad's partner, to kill Conrad's son, Paul, and daughter, Taylor, who were hiding there until Reed could be captured. Both Mitch and his wife, Elaine, however, were overpowered by Reed and seriously injured. Luckily, Paul, Conrad's twenty year old son, a student at Ohio State University, was able to get the upperhand and overcome Reed by beating him with a bat. The Neubauers and Reed were hospitalized with serious injuries but weeks later the Neubauers were recovering and thankful to be alive.

Reed finds himself in Summit County Court to face charges for the abduction and murder of Cynthia Conrad and a deer hunter, Brady Randolph, who was in the wrong place at the wrong time.

Traumatized by Quinton Reed and the loss of Cynthia, the Conrad family is trying to put the pieces of their lives together and come to terms with this senseless tragedy.

CHAPTER 1

Ivy Chandler stood at her kitchen sink washing the few dishes she and Bill had dirtied from their late dinner. As she looked out the window at their expansive backyard, she thought she saw a shadow moving behind some of her Burkwood viburnum shrubs that had grown to ten feet. She continued to stare, watching for movement again. Bill, her husband of sixteen years, walked into the kitchen and saw her staring at something. He walked up from behind her and put his arms around her waist and gave her a hug. She jumped with surprise as she was so intent on watching the bushes that she hadn't even sensed he was there.

"So what are you looking at out there?" he said.

"I thought I saw a shadow—like someone was behind the bushes and watching our house."

Bill looked outside and focused on where Ivy had directed his attention. Together they looked for a few minutes but saw nothing.

"It was probably just the wind that cast a shadow from one of our trees that gave you that impression, honey. I'm going to turn the hot tub on, and I'll look around while I'm out there. I think your eyes are playing tricks on you."

Ivy gave him an "I don't think so" look, but she couldn't explain what she thought she saw. It was a quick glimpse, and it was only a shadow. Bill was probably right, but she had never particularly liked living so far away from neighbors. They really weren't that far away, separated by a shallow woods on each side, but you couldn't really see the houses through the woods except during winter time. All the neighbors were friendly and would do anything for you if you needed help. There had never been a known problem with voyeurs, but she had been on edge for a while. This was not the first time she had seen shadows in their backyard.

Bill walked out onto their vast three—tiered deck. He looked around as he headed to the top tier to their hot tub. He saw or heard nothing out of the ordinary. He bent over and turned the hot tub on and checked the chemical content of the water. It seemed fine. Almost every evening after dinner, he and Ivy sat in the hot tub and relaxed. They enjoyed the quality time. It was their love language. They discussed world and local events, family concerns, vacation plans, their finances and investments, their jobs, and anything and everything in between. They were truly a great match, and Bill felt fortunate to have Ivy in his life these past sixteen years.

Lately, it seemed that Ivy had been a little nervous. She had mentioned that the phone had rung at various times of the day. When she would answer it, someone was definitely there but wouldn't talk. They had never invested in all the telephone company offerings. Neither had felt they needed all those bells and whistles with caller ID, call waiting, and whatever else technology could come up with. They could well afford it, but they preferred to lead a more simple life. Perhaps now caller ID would come in handy and it might indicate where the call was originating. Bill thought that he would give the phone company a call first thing next week and perhaps add some of those features. Mostly to give Ivy peace of mind.

There had been several times he found her looking out the window, looking curiously at some place in their yard. When he questioned her about it, she would just say it was nothing, that she was just looking out. He felt she was seeing something or, at least, thought she was seeing something. Whatever she was looking at, she was reticent to acknowledge it. He thought that maybe since she was moving into menopause, that might be the cause of these few moments of what seemed to him to be slight paranoia, but then, what did he know? It had never become a problem. Ivy was always very independent and never seemed to be afraid when he had to go away on a business trip. It was just lately that she had shown some signs of apprehension.

He had lived in this house twenty-two years before he married Ivy. In all of that time, his home had been broken into once. He didn't keep much money in the house and he had very little jewelry, so the burglars took very little. Nevertheless, he invested immediately in a security system. That put his mind at ease. He and Ivy always put the alarm system on before leaving for work and at night just before bedtime.

Before marrying him, Ivy had been used to living in the suburbs, where neighbors' houses were fairly close together and you could basically talk to them while mowing the lawn or getting your mail in. She enjoyed the camaraderie. She missed that living in his house, but she truly enjoyed the serene atmosphere and being out in a wooded area with lots of wildlife which this location offered.

Ivy went upstairs and quickly slipped into her bathing suit. Bill was already sitting in the hot tub waiting for her. He took her hand as she stepped into the tub and assisted her to her usual seat. She smiled at him. He was always so chivalrous. That was one thing that had attracted her to him when they first met.

"Oooh! This feels so good," she sighed.

"Yes, the temperature is perfect," he responded.

They sat under the starlit skies discussing how beautiful and calm the night was. A slight warm breeze added to their comfort. In two weeks, they were planning to fly to Hawaii for a two week vacation. Because Ivy was a high school teacher, they were pretty much restricted to summer vacations. Both were excited about the trip. They had researched the various islands and planned to start in Honolulu and visit Pearl Harbor and climb Diamond Head, then fly to Maui and enjoy some snorkeling and a luau, see the garden island, Kaui, and finally end on the big island of Hawaii and see some of the volcanoes. Ivy had researched the islands on the computer and had obtained many brochures from their travel agent, so after lengthy discussions, they had mapped out their desired activities and where they would be staying on each island. It had been two years since they had actually taken a sight-seeing vacation. Other vacation time had been spent visiting out of state relatives and enjoying their extended families or working around their house doing some upgrading. They had also gone on a mission tour with a group from their church. So they would be enjoying Hawaii during their seventeenth wedding anniversary.

As they were talking, the lights in the house suddenly went dark.

"We must have blown a fuse," stated Bill. *"I wonder what caused that?"*

"Hmmm! I don't know. The wind isn't strong enough to cause a problem."

"You stay here, and I'll go downstairs and see what's going on with the circuit breaker."

"Okay. Don't forget to grab the flashlight there by the phone."

"Okay."

Bill walked to the phone and felt for the flashlight but couldn't find it. It apparently wasn't in its usual spot. He knew the house so well, he really could find his way in the dark, but the flashlight would have helped. Rather than go out into the garage to get the other one, he didn't feel the necessity. He could feel his way downstairs and go to the circuit breaker. In fact, he had a flashlight sitting on the corner of his desk downstairs. He would just grab that one.

He managed to get downstairs with no problem and walked in total darkness to his desk. He felt for the flashlight, found it, but the light seemed rather dim. The battery must be going bad. He made his way to the back room of their basement and to the corner where the circuit breaker was. He started to open the door of the breaker box when he heard a noise coming from around the furnace. He turned quickly to see a flashlight pointed at him and the person holding the lit flashlight. But that wasn't the only thing pointed at him.

"What —" was all he had time to say.

Two bullets from a .38 Special Smith and Wesson with a silencer pierced through his heart. Bill dropped to the concrete floor, water still dripping from his swim trunks.

CHAPTER 2

Ivy had waited what seemed to be a reasonable time and still Bill hadn't been able to get the lights back on. She decided to make her way downstairs to see if she could help him or see what was going on. She wrapped her beach towel around her body and tried to dry off the best she could. She walked into the kitchen and yelled down to Bill. He must not have heard her for he didn't reply. He must have taken the flashlight because it wasn't by the phone. Since he had the flashlight and she didn't, she had to make her way down the stairs in the dark. The air condition was on in the house, and now she was starting to shiver.

"Bill? What's going on, hon? I'm coming down, but I don't see any lights on. Do you have the flashlight on?"

No response from him. Where could he have gone? She clung to the wall for guidance. She was walking to the backroom where the circuit breaker was, to see if Bill was there and just couldn't hear her speaking to him. She saw a glimmer of the flashlight before she actually walked into the room. As soon as she stepped back into there, she saw the flashlight on the floor and Bill was spread out on the floor awkwardly.

Her first thought was that he had a heart attack. Her second thought was that he could have been electrocuted. She didn't know. After all, he was wet.

In total fear, she rushed to his side and called out his name.

"Bill! Bill! Oh my God, what has happened?"

Just then a movement came from behind her—from behind the furnace. She looked up and saw the flashlight and the gun. No time to think or react. She tried standing upright.

"What are you . . ."

Two shots were fired into her head. One right between her beautiful blue eyes. The other one in the middle of her forehead. She slumped over on her back across Bill's body, with her face pointing to the ceiling. Her eyes remained opened and the shocked look was paralyzed on her face.

The Chandlers would not be going to Hawaii.

CHAPTER 3

Conrad Confidential Investigative Services had been conceived fifteen years ago by Doug Conrad. He left the Akron Police Department as a detective after seven years of service and an unblemished record. He enjoyed the investigative part of his job so much, he decided to go into business for himself.

As business flourished, his former partner with the Akron department agreed to come work for him. While Mitch Neubauer was not part owner because of his own choice, he was nevertheless treated as an equal partner and paid exceedingly well. Doug and Mitch were as close as brothers and their trust level toward the other was incomparable.

The Akron Police Department's detective bureau was recently gutted from twenty-five officers to fewer than a half dozen because of budget restraints, necessitating outsourcing so their own patrol officers weren't taken away from their normal duties. Because their schedules couldn't be flexible, they couldn't meet with victims or eye-witnesses soon enough, thus, crime trails would go cold which was crucial to any case.

The Akron Police Department had nothing but respect for Doug Conrad, one of their own, and knew that if they could hand over some of their cases to Doug, he would share information he had found with their detectives and solve cases more quickly. There was cooperation not competition among them and that was actually a rarity in their business. Some detectives were *hotshots,* trying to earn notoriety, claiming all the credit. Doug Conrad, up until the time his own wife was abducted and murdered, was a hard-working, low profile detective. Cynthia Conrad's case had made national news, so Doug Conrad's name now roused instant recognition as well as sympathy. That instant recognition for a sometimes undercover detective could now work to his detriment.

The investigative caseload in Summit County was so heavy and getting increasingly burdensome, and Doug Conrad had been out of commission for awhile during his wife and daughter's abduction and the eventual and ultimate murder of his wife. His partner, Mitch, had been shot, and his wife, Elaine, had been severely assaulted by Quinton Reed, the perpetrator, while they were temporarily protecting Conrad's two college-aged children.

Reed's trial would soon be drawing to a conclusion and, hopefully, Doug and Mitch could find closure and move on. Doug and Mitch were not the kind to want pity or sympathy. They were not easily distracted, but this heart-breaking case was overwhelming not only to the local community in which they lived but to the nation, and the healing process would take awhile.

Doug had buried his wife some months back and had returned to work. After all, he was putting his two children through college at the same time. Paul was a biology student now in his third year at Ohio State University. His daughter, Taylor, was in her second year at Kent State University. But more than that, he needed to get back to a life of normalcy and try to take his mind off the life-changing experience this family tragedy had been for him and his children.

Both Paul and Taylor had gone through counseling and seemed to be managing their grief and dealing with the frightening ordeal Quinton Reed and his son, Kevin, had put them through.

One of Doug's best friends, Pastor Jim Pascoe, dropped over to the house numerous times to visit with Doug. He was a great friend and even better support system for him. Jim and his wife had him over for dinner at least once a month. Like Cynthia, she was a wonderful cook. As he observed the sweet interaction between Jim and Holly, he realized how much he missed being married and having someone to talk to or laugh with.

CHAPTER 4

Two weeks ago, Quinton Reed had been found guilty by a jury of his peers. His was a capital case. And now, at sentencing, Quinton Reed was permitted to have people provide mitigating circumstances to beg for life with no possibility of parole rather than the death penalty. He had no one willing to speak on his behalf.

Family members of the victim were permitted to speak to the defendant and share their thoughts about Reed's punishment. The Conrad family appeared in the courtroom in solidarity. Paul Conrad and Taylor stood separately at the podium and described their mother to Quinton and to the judge. With brevity but deep emotion they shared what their mother's relationship had meant to them and the loss they felt and will always feel. Both tried unsuccessfully to hold back the tears. Both asked for the full rigors of the law.

Finally, Doug Conrad stood to give the final testimony and request.

"My wife was beautiful. As lovely as she was on the outside, she was ten times lovelier on the inside." All of the overwhelming emotions of Cynthia's abduction and murder welled up inside Doug. He felt such a deep void in his life these past few months—a void that would never again be filled.

"She had so much to give to our family, to her many friends, and our church. She reached out to those in need. She was a loving person, and you tortured her and then shot her in the back. It was a cold-blooded, calculated murder. You seem to have a cold heart as well. You reap what you sow, Mr. Reed. You had choices, and you chose the ones that would one day bring you demise as well. In the end, God will be your final

judge, and I hope that you will make your peace with Him, but while on earth, you have a debt that must be paid.

"I hate the word 'widower,' but that's what I am now because of you. You have altered the life and happiness of my children, my business partner and his wife, and Brady Randolph's family by your malicious and wicked intents. You have hurt too many people.

While I hope you find spiritual redemption, I don't feel you deserve to be redeemed on this earth. I believe in "an eye for an eye," and while I take no pleasure in saying this, 'you do deserve to die."

Doug then took his gaze off Quinton and looked straight at Judge Daniels:

"I ask that Quinton Reed be sentenced to the full rigor of the law with no mercy shown, Your Honor."

He returned to his seat. He took the hands of both his son and his daughter and gave each of them a nervous squeeze.

Judge Daniels asked the defendant to rise. Quinton stood. He already knew his future was doomed. His lawyer had prepared him for the worst and most likely scenario. Since he had nothing to lose, he realized that somewhere down the road, he would need a plan.

"Quinton Reed, you reigned terror for over five days on the Conrad family, Mitch and Elaine Neubauer, and Brady Randolph. You negatively influenced your own son and nearly killed him. You are a detriment to society and anyone who is in your path. Therefore, this court sentences you to death by way of lethal injection on . . ."

Taylor Conrad let out a loud sob—albeit a sob of affirmation of the judge's decision. Doug held on to her as she sobbed uncontrollably. Paul had his arm around his dad and part of Taylor's shoulder. Nothing would bring their mom back. Nothing. But justice was fairly served in this courtroom. Why, then, didn't this moment feel like a victory? It was finally over—this whole sordid mess. Mom could finally rest in peace and Quinton Reed would never hurt anyone else ever again!

The judge slammed the gavel on his desk. As the Conrads were walking out of the courtroom, Quinton watched them and thought, "See ya around, Conrad. See ya around!"

CHAPTER 5

Weeks had passed and Doug was closing two of his cases. Since his unwanted national popularity, Jean, his secretary, couldn't keep up with all of the calls from prospective clients. Doug certainly needed to keep busy, but in order to service more clients, he needed to hire at least one more detective. Doug was always selective about the cases his company accepted. He and Mitch limited their investigative work to civil, criminal, and corporate cases. Occasionally they took on missing persons. His detectives were licensed, bonded, and professional.

Mitch affirmed the need to post a position. They set up the criteria and had an employment agency shop for prospects who matched the job description.

inally, a detective for the Charlottesville Police Department in ottesville, Virginia, for over twenty years.

an escorted the forty-one-year-old woman into Doug's office rose from his chair and walked around his desk to greet her. g read her job history, he had expected her to be a large framed, ry type woman. Quite the contrary. She was a lovely, elegant, and blonde who stood no taller than five feet three inches. She had a handshake and a beautiful smile. She was dressed in a black suit, blouse, and conservative two inch high heels. Her jewelry was e but striking. She certainly didn't match the stereotype of most rmed detectives he had known over the years.

oug had never given much thought to the gender for detectives ng for him but admittedly assumed they would be men. Physical na was a must, and he needed to be sure they were able to *"cover other's back."* They needed to be strong emotionally as well.

he was seated and once he returned to his seat, the interview n. As the questions progressed, he learned that she had been ed for twenty years until her husband, Pete, died of pancreatic r, ten months after the diagnosis. They had sought help from rous medical institutions and tried an experimental treatment could possibly buy him some extra time. None of their efforts successful, but she agreed they grasped for every straw they l get.

er seventy-five year old mother, Stella, lived in Akron and would ually need some over-seeing, so she decided to sell their home in nia and move to the Akron area to be with her mom.

s they moved into a discussion about her training, she produced f her certifications, proving she had been on the SWAT team and g the various weapons she was trained to use. She shared some of ases she had worked on as a police officer that put her in harm's way to moving into the detective division. She promised her mother she d remain a detective to reduce her chances of being in dangerous gs. Doug could certainly appreciate that.

CHAPTER 6

Today was dedicated to interviewing candida
detective. The first candidate was a young man nar
He was at least six feet five inches tall and terribly
good training but little experience. He seemed a little
His height would definitely draw attention to himse
detectives working undercover want. On occasion,
work to his advantage.

The next candidate came with more training,
training, and job experience. His name was Barnab
an average-height, dark-skinned African American
personality and a big laugh as he shared a few of h
military policeman. Doug connected with him imn
handled himself with finesse and professionalism th
interview. After the interview concluded, Doug sent I
office for a second interview.

Several more candidates were interviewed but I
to be a good match for Conrad Confidential. One n
scheduled for today: a female named Donna Gifford.

As he reviewed her résumé, he had to admit he v
with her background and experience. She was wid
moved to the Akron area from Virginia after having b

He also noticed her resume indicated she had a black belt in judo. She supplied a list of professional references and three letters of recommendation, one from her previous employer. Everything seemed authentic, but she seemed to be too feminine. Could she be everything these papers say she is? Could she cover someone's back and keep her wits about her? He had gone through his list of questions, and her responses surpassed his expectations.

He asked Donna to stand and show any weapons she was carrying. She opened her blazer and holstered was her PM 9 Kahr with its Laser Sight. In her purse was a canister of Mace.

He then asked her to step to an open area in his office. He decided to set up a role-playing scenario. He began to set the scene: you have just come upon an armed murderer who just discovered you are a cop and . . .

The next thing Doug knew he was lying on his back looking up with the high heel of her left shoe pressed into his esophagus. Donna Gifford was a woman he wouldn't want to run into on a sunny afternoon much less a dark night.

Somewhat embarrassed and at the same time apologetic, she removed her foot from his neck and helped him up. He should have seen that coming, but it is the element of surprise that gives you the advantage. She definitely knew what she was doing and could hold her own. She began to wipe his shirt near his tie knot; he assumed she was brushing off her footprint from his white shirt.

Sheepishly, Doug acknowledged her sharp, anticipatory instincts. He had also noticed she had quickly spotted his fall, making sure he didn't get hurt.

"I'm sorry, Mr. Conrad. Sometimes men in our business hesitate utilizing women for fear we can't take care of ourselves much less be an equal and protective partner to them, but we can. I'm assuming that's where you were going with your little scenario. I trained right alongside the men, and, yes, while the genders differ in size and strength, we can bring things to the table that men in the field can't, so we all have our place."

"I have no doubt that is correct, Mrs. Gifford. Could I escort you down the hall for a second interview with my partner, Mitch Neubauer?"

She followed him to Mitch's office. He returned to his office and called Mitch, knowing Gifford was sitting right in front of him.

"Whatever you do, don't set up any role-playing. I'm convinced she could kill both of us at the same time with little effort."

Mitch, unsure what made Doug call and share that right then, merely smiled and hung up the phone.

CHAPTER 7

At the end of the day, Mitch and Doug discussed each one of the candidates, narrowing them down to Barnabus Johnson and Donna Gifford.

Mitch felt the same way about Barnabus Johnson as Doug did. He also laughed at many things Barnabus told him; so besides being competent, he would be fun to work with.

When they began discussing Donna Gifford, Doug shared with Mitch his role-playing scenario that went awry. Mitch curled over in his chair laughing. Doug looked rather amused himself while telling it. Mitch knew that Doug didn't have such a big ego that he couldn't laugh at himself, but perhaps he was a bit bemused at how she got the upper hand of him so quickly.

Mitch didn't want to seem overly eager about choosing Donna, but he was mesmerized by her beauty and brains. She was the *whole package.* Sometimes it would prove beneficial to use a woman for some of their assignments. Another thought that crossed his mind but that he would never verbalize to Doug was that she reminded him so much of Cynthia. Donna was sophisticated and even elegant and yet down to earth. Doug was nowhere near looking for a mate, but wouldn't it be nice to have Donna nearby as a *"friend?"*

CHAPTER 8

Each day Jean, Doug's secretary, was getting more and more flustered by the myriad calls pouring in. It seemed like everyone felt they knew Doug Conrad personally from his TV appearances during his family tragedy. They trusted him and respected his family values. Doug Conrad always handled himself professionally and with a kind and caring demeanor and that came across. Therefore, he was in demand as an investigator.

They actually felt the same way about Mitch Neubauer who had been described on TV and in the paper as a hero to the Conrad children. He became an icon in Summit County.

Jean was having to turn away cases that they would normally have accepted, but there weren't enough agents to handle them. Doug was fielding many of the calls himself. He never took on more cases than his company could handle. He always gave himself some availability should there be a priority case come to their attention—either presented by the Akron and Summit County police or a private individual. He accepted mostly challenging cases.

Doug had wanted to eventually expand the business but had not felt the time was right. Eventually Doug's popularity would wane and his fame, if you could call it that, would be short-lived. At least he hoped so, but while the workload was thriving and his financial resources were soaring, he thought it prudent to perhaps hire two more detectives and accept more cases. His goal for the company had always been to start small and then enlarge as business picked up. It was evident the time had come.

Before the end of the day and after much discussion, Doug with Mitch's strong input, decided to hire both Barnabus Johnson and Donna Gifford.

CHAPTER 9

Helen Porter and her adult daughter Alayna Fisher had a one o'clock appointment with Doug Conrad. They were prepared to hire Mr. Conrad to find out who had murdered their daughter and sister, Ivy Chandler, along with her husband, Bill.

The Summit County sheriff's office had been working on the case, but it was evident it had moved to a cold case. They were told that murder cases are usually solved within the first week of the murder, but there was hardly any evidence obtained at the crime scene and no obvious motive. The deputies were understaffed and overworked and Helen, a widow, and her divorced daughter, Alayna, pooled their money together to hire a private detective.

Doug remembered reading about the case in the newspaper and hearing the reports on television. It was an intriguing case, he thought at the time.

Both the mother and sister seemed to have memorized every detail of the case and presented the facts in a very organized fashion. Their pain was obvious, and their desire to find the killer or killers and to learn the motive was paramount to them and, understandably so. Up until now Doug had never been able to fully realize the depth of pain relatives of murder victims felt. Now he could truly empathize.

"Do you have any thoughts about who would have murdered them or why?" Doug asked the two women.

"No ideas whatsoever. They were a sweet, loving couple. They loved the family and were loved by us. They had lots of friends. There were no known enemies. If anything was stolen from their house, we couldn't tell."

Doug accepted the case and assured them he would thoroughly review the police reports and begin working on the case. Both provided their phone numbers where they could be reached. With tears in their eyes, they shook Doug's hand and thanked him.

CHAPTER 10

Because of Quinton Reed's violent background and capital death sentence, the Akron Police Department opted to use a professional and official law enforcement agency to transport him from the Akron jail to the Ohio State Penitentiary in Youngstown, Ohio where all male death row prisoners are housed before moving to the Southern Ohio Correctional Facility in Lucasville where the actual execution would take place.

The Interstate Transportation of Dangerous Criminals Act of 2000 required specific regulations relating to the transporting of violent prisoners by the transporting agency. Generally, specially designed prisoner transport vehicles are equipped with security features to prevent escapes and any dangerous implications to the transporting security personnel. Some transports will go as far as to wear protective gears like helmets, stab resistant gloves, and protective gas masks. Usually prisoners are deterred from planning an escape when they see how well equipped the transport officers are.

Actual restrictions on the number of hours that transport agents could be on duty are spelled out. In the event of an escape by a violent prisoner, the agents are required to immediately notify the appropriate law enforcement officials in the jurisdiction where the escape occurs. It also provides civil penalties of $10,000 for a violation of such regulations, in addition to the costs of prosecution. It also mandates restitution to any entity of the state which had to expend funds for the sole purpose of apprehending any violent prisoner who escaped from a transport agency as the result of neglect or a violation of regulations. As a result of this act, agents take every precaution possible. Their personal safety could be in jeopardy as well, so all the more reason to follow all of the safety rules mandated.

Several phone calls and meetings with the hired transport agency had resulted in the time and method of transport. It was agreed upon that Reed would wear the bright—orange jail jumpsuit that would clearly identify him as a prisoner. For the safety of all Ohio citizens, it was decided he would be transported at midnight on a weekday when highway traffic would be scarce. Arrival time would be at approximately 1:04 a.m. as Youngstown was only 59.17 miles from Akron, and a one hour, four minute drive. Every minute detail was considered.

Reed was slowly recovering from two broken arms and a concussion after Doug Conrad's son beat him with a bat while fighting to defend his life and that of his sister, Taylor. There was no question Reed was considered a noncooperative prisoner. Even as bad of shape as he was in, he would try to escape and wreak havoc on anyone who got in his way if he was given even half a chance. Summit County officials were going to do everything in their power to see that Quinton Reed didn't escape and would meet his date with death.

Given an updated and thorough medical report on Quinton Reed's own injuries and recent surgeries with his physical limitations, the two transport agents, Buford Stanley and Corbin Daniels (no relation to Judge Daniels) felt this would be an easy transport. It wouldn't be necessary to wear the helmets, gloves, or gas masks. No need for overkill. Ordinarily Reed would have been restrained with handcuffs behind his back, but because of his broken arms and lack of mobility, he would need to be cuffed to a belly chain in front of his body. But he would be cuffed. He would be girded with a transportation belt and they would add restraints to his ankles. Reed wasn't going anywhere.

CHAPTER 11

For three hours Doug had been perusing the voluminous files on Bill and Ivy Chandler. Doug decided to pull Mitch, Barnabus, and Donna in on this case. He would like to see this case solved as quickly as possible for the sake of this family and for justice. The longer it went unsolved, the colder the trail would get.

He gave Mitch, Barnabus, and Donna each a thick file to read through and then they were to meet back in an hour with a summary of their file. Donna Gifford had a college degree in behavioral science which gave her a better understanding of *who* criminals are, *how* they think, and *why* they do what they do. That knowledge in itself would be a tremendous help in solving crimes and preventing attacks. She studied in depth the art of *profiling*, the management of death investigations, psycho-social behavior, and the spirituality of criminals.

Barnabus, on the other hand, was highly trained at the FBI Academy on a Marine Corps base in Quantico, Virginia about thirty-six miles outside Washington, D.C. It is a premier learning and research center where the best practices throughout the global criminal justice community are taught. Doug and Mitch were trained there at the same time also but over twenty-two years ago. It is a place where lasting partnerships are forged among law enforcement and intelligence professionals. So Mitch and Doug knew the kind of rigorous training Barnabus had undergone. The military background of the three men with a woman's intuition and state of the art training among all four could almost guarantee this case being solved, no matter how tough it looked.

CHAPTER 12

The hour was up and Donna, Barnabus, Mitch, and Doug gathered around the conference table.

"*Who wants to go first?*" asked Doug.

"*I will,*" responded Mitch. "*My file provided mostly personal background about the couple.*

"*Ivy and Bill Chandler were married for sixteen, almost seventeen years. It was a second marriage for Bill but a first for Ivy. Bill had been married to a woman named Rita Marie Morgan. They were married for only five years and had a son named Andrew. It was anything but an amicable divorce.*

"*It is believed that Rita had an extra-marital affair with a neighbor and family friend. Thus, the divorce. Rita did end up marrying the neighbor, but it tore up the lives of two families.*

"*The first Mrs. Chandler denied the affair, but eight months after the break up, she married Chaz Darrington. There were many witnesses who could confirm the affair despite Rita's denial.*

"*Rita Chandler Darrington and her husband, Chaz, had proven alibis on the night of the murders, so authorities eliminated them pretty quickly as suspects. They have been happily married for twenty years supposedly and had no contact with Bill Chandler after Andrew was nineteen years old and the support checks were stopped.*

"Andrew—he goes by Andy—is now twenty-five years old. He too was questioned by police. He had had no contact with his father or stepmother since the age of fifteen."

"Why was that?" asked Donna.

"Apparently he had issues with the stepmom and didn't like going over to his dad's house. All of his friends were in Ellet where he grew up. It was the typical feelings of a kid from a divorced home."

"Did he have an alibi?" asked Donna.

"Not a good one, really. He said he was at his apartment watching TV. He lives alone, had worked all day, and was tired.

"No one could actually confirm that, but police confirmed he was at work that day and that he had stopped at a McDonald's for a pick up on his way home.

The boy is polite, cleancut, with no criminal record whatsoever. Friends, teachers, his employer and employees had nothing but nice things to say about him."

"Did the boy attend his father's funeral?" asked Donna.

"He went to the visiting hours but not the funeral as Bill and Ivy's funeral were officiated by the same pastor at the same time."

"What about the ex-wife?" asked Donna.

"No, she didn't attend visiting hours or the funeral."

"Was the son named in the will?" asked Doug.

"No, but he didn't expect to be, according to Andy, since he had had no relationship with his dad for years."

Donna lifted her eyebrows. "Hmmmm."

Everyone around the table looked at her.

"Who was the executor of the will?" Barnabus asked.

"Ivy's sister," responded Doug. "Bill had two out of state siblings and with that and because of the age of his elderly mother at the time, it made more sense to use Alayna, the nearest sibling."

"So who benefited from the will and how much money are we talking about?" said Doug as he guided their thinking . . .

Barnabus cleared his throat.

CHAPTER 13

"*Well, that's where I believe my file comes in,*" responded Barnabus.

"*Mr. Chandler owned his own business, Chandler Corbox. He owned a corrugated and fiber box company in the industrial section on S. Main Street in downtown Akron. They make boxes of all kinds and sizes and ship all over the world. Mr. Chandler traveled to Hong Kong, Singapore, Thailand, and Japan quite often on business.*

"*He seemed to be highly respected and admired by the employees. He was the kind of owner who cared about his factory workers, their safety, and he worked right alongside them when the need called for it. He mostly handled sales and contracts, but he got his start working in a box factory when he was a teen. He worked part-time there all through his college days as well. He studied business administration at the University of Akron, earned his M.B.A. and started Chandler Corbox with the financial help of his parents and Fifth Third.*

"*It's a non-union company. Police tried to find some disgruntled employees, looking for a motive, but couldn't seem to find anything significant. Records indicate there wasn't a big turnover at Corbox.*

"*The business was in good standing within the community, it was functioning in the black, according to the accountant, and profits were healthy.*

"*Mr. Chandler's tax records show he earned about $300,000 a year.*"

41

"Wow! Who would have thunk the cardboard box business was that good?" commented Mitch.

"All right, so we couldn't find anything that would besmirch the reputation of Bill Chandler?" asked Doug.

"None. Police couldn't find anyone who denigrated this man. He was a sweet dude!" remarked Barnabus.

"Well, here is a man of power who was well liked. Women would probably find him very attractive. Any known affairs?" asked Donna.

"We might want to pursue that, but nothing in the records to indicate one was found."

"A spurned woman can be treacherous," Donna continued.

"So what about Ivy?" Doug inquired.

"Ivy was a year younger than Bill. She had never been married before. She taught high school math for nearly eighteen years. Worked around kids all day. Never hit bars or single hangouts. Was a churchgoer. Saw some of her school pictures, and she was a real looker!" Barnabus smiled.

"School administrators said she was a no-nonsense teacher in the classroom, very efficient, and respected among the students."

"Did she have many discipline problems with students? Perhaps boys with a crush on her?" asked Donna.

"Well, there were crushes on her, for sure, over the years, but if she was aware of them, she never let on. Her character was above reproach, according to her colleagues.

She was a real 'sweet pea!' * smiled Barnabus. *"It's a shame she died the way she did.*

"The school held a memorial for her in the gym. She was eulogized by many of the students, administrators, and colleagues. Counselors were brought in to the school to help deal with her death.

"She was thrilled when she became engaged to Bill Chandler. The staff was so happy for her. They described her marriage as a 'match made in heaven.' They were compatible and attended many social events together.

"Ivy graduated from Malone College in secondary education and earned a Masters degree in counseling. She earned $72,000 a year and had an annuity of $80,000 through a company with the school. So yes, between her salary and Bill's, they brought in about $372,000 a year. They were living comfortably.

"Prior to getting married, she was a counselor at her church's youth camp for teens during her summer hiatus and participated in the Big Sister organization. She cared about young people and seemed like a genuine, caring person.

"So everyone questioned by police were baffled that anyone would want to kill her," concluded Barnabus.

CHAPTER 14

"*Well, someone wanted her dead. Two bullets placed between her eyes at close range indicates whoever did this wanted to make sure she never walked out of that basement alive,*" commented Donna.

"*I guess that brings us to the medical examiner's report, the autopsy, and a final assessment from Dr. Brandon White, the psychological criminal profiler for the Summit County Sheriff's Department.*

"*Bill Chandler was murdered first, based on the position of the bodies. He was shot in their basement — in the chest twice, one bullet piercing his aorta and the second bullet pierced his left ventricle. A Smith and Wesson Bodyguard .380 was used. He was found wearing swim trunks with a beach towel wrapped around his waist. Apparently he and Ivy had been in their hot tub prior to going to the basement. Something took both of them downstairs. Both were found in the farthest back room near the circuit breaker. A flashlight was found beside Bill's body, so it was believed he was holding it at the time. Given the location, it would seem they had lost power in the house. Digital clocks were blinking throughout the house. It is believed someone was hiding downstairs and pulled the power switch in order to lure the Chandlers downstairs.*

"*Mr. Chandler's body position appeared he had turned from the circuit breaker, so he might have heard something. Since no struggle occurred, the perpetrator totally surprised him, getting off his two lethal shots at close range. A silencer was more than likely used.*

"A very short time later, Ivy goes downstairs and perhaps walking in the dark to find Bill. She, too, was in a bathing suit. It appears she bent down, then tried to stand upright—more than likely she, too, heard or saw something, but was shot before she could react.

"Both died suddenly, so there was little blood at the scene. It's possible one or both got a look at their killer and that they may have even known the person or persons, although it looks like there was only one perp.

"The killer was no more than four feet from the victims when he or she fired the gun. Even a bad shooter should be able to hit the target at such close range, and yet he or she was far enough away to not risk the chance of a physical encounter and leaving evidence in their wake.

"The killer was using the .380 Smith and Wesson, as I said. It has a built in laser. No casings or shells were found at the scene.

"Now the question is, how could the perp get inside the Chandler home? ADT records show their alarm system was not engaged at the time. Since there was no sign of forced entry, it's possible one of them left a door to their house unlocked.

"Or the perp had a key," interjected Barnabus.

"Right," said Donna.

"There were no known witnesses. Neighbors who don't really have a view of the Chandler home saw or heard nothing that evening. All seemed shocked to learn of their murders. There was no dissension between Chandlers and any of their neighbors.

"Money and jewelry were found untouched in the bedroom. Their wallets were found on the bedroom dressers in full view and the safe in the bedroom closet had not been tampered with.

"Authorities checked their computer for e-mails but nothing raised their eyebrows or got their attention.

"Dr. White suggests it has to be either a family member with a vendetta who knew the layout of the house and the daily routine of the Chandlers OR a serial killer who stumbled upon either Bill or Ivy and followed him or her home and waited for the opportunity to strike.

"I concur with his first suggestion about a family member. Killers usually always have a motive for killing. They know WHO they want dead and WHY. They justify it in their mind.

"If it is the former, then we need to find the motive, which should lead us straight to the killer or killers. My experience tells me we need to find a money trail. The Chandlers led a pretty normal, comfortable life. They were down to earth people, but they crossed somebody."

That comment caused pause around the table. It was a sobering thought.

CHAPTER 15

Doug's file pertained to the Chandlers' finances and will.

"As you said, Barnabus, their last IRS return indicated a joint gross income of $372,000. The Chandler's paid their bills on time and lived within their financial means. They gave generously to many different charities: American Cancer Society, Haven of Rest, American vets, scholarship funds to their universities, and tithed at their church.

"Their bank accounts, both savings and checking, contained generous amounts in them. The killer had the opportunity to remove the monies out of the ATM machine, although it would have been risky, and didn't, so money doesn't seem to be the motive in this case.

"They had sizable investments with Raymond James Associates and had separate annuities within their own companies. Both had excellent health and retirement benefits and, according to medical records and the autopsy, both were in excellent health up to the time of their sudden deaths.

"Other than their house mortgage, they had no other outstanding loans. Neither were gamblers, drinkers, or drug users.

"They had living wills which indicated their desire to donate their body organs or any part that could be used upon their death. Unfortunately, their bodies weren't found in time for that.

"They had a social circle of about four other couples with whom they were quite close to, and the rest of their social life revolved around family.

"In answer to the beneficiaries of the will, their monies clearly went to each of their siblings, to the nieces and a nephew, with a clear statement that Bill's only biological son, Andrew, was not entitled to any of the money due to his desertion from the family circle. Everyone looked around the table at one another to see their reactions.

"Ivy Chandler kept a journal for over twenty-two years. Those journals were taken into evidence, but as yet, no one has really read through those to ascertain any family problems or a concern, threat, or fear of someone.

"Donna, would you be willing to go to the sheriff's office tomorrow and see if we can get a copy of those?" Doug asked.

"Sure."

"So here is your all-American couple. The least likely couple to be murdered. So what happened, people?" Doug asked.

"Someone's expectation didn't get met perhaps?" inquired Mitch.

"Might it be a short fuse or a sudden rage case?" asked Barnabus.

"Is the serial killer theory feasible? He followed an opportunity home?" questioned Doug with skepticism.

"Did a son feel rejected, pushed out, and denied what he felt should have been his and one day just snapped?" asked Donna.

The three men looked up with some surprise at her stark comment, for Donna's thoughts were leading them down a road that none of them wanted to take.

CHAPTER 16

As soon as the transport vehicle arrived, Buford Stanley and Corbin Daniels stepped out and headed to a private area of the Summit County Jail. Neither man had any apprehension about this assignment. Over the years they had transported quite a few criminals to prison—dangerous ones—and those who were bound for death row as well. They took all the necessary precautions required of them and had never had an incident.

Buford usually did the driving while Corbin kept his eyes on their surroundings for signs of a carjacking or any ruse the criminal might try to pull. Today, however, Buford suggested he would like to ride shotgun and Corbin could drive.

Not wanting Corbin to know the real reason behind the suggestion, Buford knew he was violating one of the rules but felt it was a minor violation. He was not well rested. The night before, his wife who was an airline stewardess for AirTran was scheduled for a late flight out of the Akron Canton Airport, so he was home alone with their three kids. It worked out since his transport wasn't until the next night, and Jenny would be home by then. However, his six year old son, Nicholas, had several nightmares throughout the night and had been crying. Buford had to go into his room twice to comfort him and finally, the third time, decided to carry him into his bed for the remainder of the night.

Nick had tossed and turned and kicked almost all night long. Buford got hardly any sleep at all. Nicholas got up the next morning having no recollection of his nightmares and felt completely rested before he marched out of the house to catch his school bus.

Buford, on the other hand, felt tired and sluggish, so it was best if he not drive. The trip was only an hour long, and once Reed was turned over to the prison authorities and a few release papers were signed, he and Corbin could be on their way home. In another hour and a half, he could be home sleeping.

Three officers escorted Quinton to the bathroom before taking the elevator down to the back of the building where he would be helped into the transport vehicle. He was wearing his bright orange prison uniform and was handcuffed in the front of his body with a belly chain.

The transport agents put their special cuffs on Quinton and with the key from the Summit County deputies removed theirs and returned them. Reed's feet were fettered. The back door was shut and secured, which could only be opened from the outside. The back windows were shaded, so every security measure possible was taken.

"We will *be arriving at Ohio State Penitentiary in Youngstown, Ohio at approximately 1:10 a.m., Mr. Reed. There are no stops along the way, no matter what.*"

The vehicle was designed so that Stanley and Daniels could hear any sounds Reed made or any words spoken, but he couldn't hear theirs unless they hit an intercom button allowing them a two-way conversation. However, they would not be conversing with Reed whatsoever. Both Stanley and Daniels had watched the Conrad case play out on television and were naturally curious to meet the infamous Quinton Reed. Just to look at him one would never suspect he was a cold-blooded killer or a guy who would try to kill his own son.

Buford loved Nicholas and his twin daughters so much, he couldn't imagine anyone doing such a horrible thing. The guy was a scumbag and deserved the sentence he got, but neither Stanley nor Daniels would verbalize their true feelings to Reed or attempt to incite him. They were professionals and, besides, it was company policy as well.

Legally Reed couldn't be tied to anything inside the vehicle so he had room to find comfortable positions despite his hands cuffed in front and his feet fettered. Quinton looked out the window as the vehicle pulled away from the jailhouse on Crosier Street.

When the car turned onto Interstate 76 east, the vehicle picked up speed to fifty-five miles per hour. Soundproof glass separated the front seat from the back. Quinton could see the agents talking, but he couldn't hear a word they were saying. He tried to lip read when one would turn his head to the side, but he could only catch a word now and then. Nothing he could follow, so he amused himself by looking at the sights familiar to him—Hoban High School on the hill, Goodyear Tire & Rubber Company, the exit for Kent State University where Taylor Conrad was attending. Too bad, he thought. He would have had quite a time with her if he had gotten his hands on that pretty young thing.

As they got out a little farther on the highway, the speed limit picked up to 65 m.p.h. and so did their vehicle. Quinton had already checked the back doors to see if he could open them. He couldn't. If he was going to escape, it would have to take place enroute to prison. Once in the confines of the prison building and under the scrutiny of the guards, it would be all but impossible.

Quinton sat in silence thinking of any and every ruse he could that might allow for an escape. With a death sentence, he had nothing to lose and everything to gain IF he could escape.

As they moved further east and out of the city limits into a more remote portion of the trip, Quinton took a slouched position. There were no street lights on the side of the highway and lots of wooded areas after they passed West Branch. He remembered taking this same route with Cynthia Conrad in the trunk of his car some months back. He laid his head on the back of the seat and closed his eyes, reliving the rape in the shed. If he hadn't fallen asleep afterward, she wouldn't have escaped. He would have then killed her and would be a free man today. One mistake . . . one bad mistake . . . It was one that couldn't be rectified.

Quinton kept his eyes closed and began to allow the anger at himself to dissipate. Quinton never had much of a conscience and rarely felt guilty about most of the things he had done during his life. His one regret was shooting his son and getting a good kid—his own kid—mixed up in his crimes. He figured the court would probably give Kevin a break. After all, he got lots of breaks as a teen in juvenile court. He was in and out of trouble quite a bit—albeit they were rather petty crimes compared to what he got Kevin involved in. And, unfortunately, Kevin was nineteen years old.

With the movement of the car, the rolling sound of the tires on the highway, and the darkness, Quinton fell asleep.

CHAPTER 17

Donna Gifford had obtained a copy of Ivy Chandler's journals and had been reading them with interest for over an hour.

You learn so much from a person's writing, Donna thought. Ivy had no idea anyone would be reading her most personal and private thoughts when she penned them. Donna almost felt like she was trespassing on Ivy's heart and emotions.

Two adjectives stood out in her mind with Ivy: kind-spirited and generous. Ivy showed she cared for people in so many ways. She showed compassion to her neighbors, friends, and even relatives of her friends who passed away by preparing and delivering meals to them—not just a dish or two but entire meals. She sent numerous cards and kind notes to people. She kept in touch with her former college roommates who lived out of state and even sent money each year to one roommate who had five sons and struggled financially. She visited friends in the hospital and took the time to meet old acquaintances for lunch.

She enjoyed cooking and having friends and family over for candlelight dinners. She went to elaborate means to make houseguests feel comfortable in her home yet special all the while. She threw bridal and baby showers for her two goddaughters.

She bought something from every neighbor kid who knocked on her door selling something for a school fund raiser. She attended school functions and sports events her nieces and nephew were in whenever possible, and she gave them her time.

She kept a pristine home, hated bugs and spiders, and loved the color pink.

It seemed that Ivy was always thinking about how she could help others or what she could do for them. She was exceedingly good to her mother and sister.

She hadn't found any mention of Andrew yet. But so far, she couldn't find any reason why anyone would want to take the life of this compassionate and caring lady. Is it possible that Bill was the target and Ivy simply got in the way?

The more she read about Ivy's life and lifestyle, the more confused and perplexed she became as she searched for a clear motive for her murder. Nothing was forthcoming.

CHAPTER 18

Inside his cubicle in the office he shared with Donna Gifford, Barnabus Johnson was reading Dr. Brandon White's report, suggesting that the Chandlers could have been murdered by a possible serial killer. Dr. White's expertise in the criminal field was so highly respected, and yet Barnabus thought the theory was preposterous, based on what he knew and had studied about serial killers.

Profiling is an *art* and is one way to aid an investigation. Mistakes can be made. For instance, if the profiler doesn't truly believe what the evidence seems to show at the crime scene, he may withhold information on important profile items that could lead to an arrest. So profiling can help solve cases or it can prevent a case from being solved because everyone is on the wrong track.

Profiles are *generalizations*. Profilers like Dr. White are trained in very specific areas of crime and human nature. Criminal profilers possess a lot of knowledge and training, but they also possess a lot of pure basic instinct and that, for Barnabus, needed to be taken into consideration as well. The breadth and depth of Barnabus's background on the subject was miniscule compared to Dr. White's, however. Not wanting to leave any rock unturned, Barnabus needed to follow Dr. White's thinking on this case.

Homicide investigators usually lack the departmental support for serial killer cases, so a profiler can narrow the search of the offender greatly by letting police know what kind of person they are most likely looking for. It also can help in the interrogation process so the officer knows what questions to ask and what method to use on the suspect based on the personality type.

So Barnabus began to read Dr. White's basis for suggesting a serial killer:

> *"Serial killers take on different forms brought on by many different states of mind. Their kill is usually one on one with rare exceptions where the relationship between the victims and the offender is that of a stranger or slight acquaintance where apparent motives are lacking."*

Well, that certainly could fit this case. No clear motive had been discovered thus far, but perhaps the motive is just shrouded, thought Barnabus. However, under his training he was taught there is no such thing as a *motiveless* crime.

> *"Rarely do serial killers kill for money. They kill for the thrill of killing or for the dominance they achieve by the kill."*

It's true no money or possession seemed to have been taken from the home.

> *"Most serial killers are white males between twenty to thirty years old who target strangers near their home or place of work. Sixty-two per cent of them target strangers exclusively and usually kill people of their own race."*

Chandlers lived in a white neighborhood so a white male probably wouldn't attract any attention if seen walking around.

> *"Usually they are sociopaths with a character disorder rather than a mental disorder, but they appear so normal. They lack a conscience, feeling no remorse for their crimes. They get*

a rush by holding the power of life and death in their hands, and actually savor that feeling. If not apprehended, they will strike again. They enjoy the murder being acknowledged and feared, and while they don't seek celebrity status, they enjoy controlling the lives of thousands of area residents."

Not knowing why the Chandlers were the victims surely caused the neighbors to wonder if this was merely a random killing, and if so, could they be next?

"Serial killers can even be charming. They can con their victims by impersonating an authoritative figure with a friendly little chat."

Was Ivy somehow charmed by this man?

"If the crime scene shows evidence of careful planning, he is likely intelligent and older. Serial killers don't know their victims or have any hatred for them personally, but they might be symbolic in some way. Most of the time, the victims never did anything to hurt them in any way."

That struck a chord with Barnabus. The Chandlers appeared to be the *"perfect couple."* There is no evidence they ever hurt anyone. So why? Why?

"The serial killer is hard to catch because he tends to select vulnerable victims of some specific type who gratify his need to control people. He usually prefers to kill with hands on methods such as strangulation or stabbings, but at any given time, twenty to fifty unidentified active serial killers are at work changing their target and methods. Because they plan their murders, they often travel long distances between their crimes."

This clearly didn't seem to apply to the Chandler murders although it did appear to be planned. Could it be someone who worked for Bill Chandler and wanted to control him? Yet there were no hands on. It looked like a clean kill. You shoot, kill, and walk away. Then he hid again, shot, killed, and walked away. Did this killer procure a powerful weapon to make him feel more potent? Except in rare cases, serial killers work alone. With the weapon used on the Chandlers, there was little risk involved for him. And how do we even know we're looking for a *"him?"* This is a crime that could have clearly been committed by a female.

The FBI had always asserted that a serial killer had to complete three separate murders spaced by a duration or cooling off period that can vary from a few days to years. But they ALL must have a method to their killing. Modus operandi was the term. There was no personation or signature found in this case. So it's possible the killer had no relationship to the Chandlers.

Having reviewed the crime scene photos and report, Barnabus concluded there had been no staging either. This is where the offender alters the crime scene prior to the arrival of the police. Had that been done, it would have indicated the offender had some type of relationship with the victims. It is also used by the killer to direct the course of the investigation away from the suspect, especially if he did have a relationship with the victim or victims. So it is possible the killer had no relationship to the Chandlers. Hmmm.

"Because they kill for idiosyncratic reasons and frequently
wait months between killings, serial killers are hard to catch."

There was so much in this report to think about. Dr. White went on to say that

"there is usually a pre-crime stressor that provokes a killer
to action. The loss of a job, the break up of a relationship, and
money problems are three big crime stressors."

Given the economic complexion of Akron right now, many people had lost their jobs. Lots of people were unemployed right now and having money problems.

The break up of a relationship? So is it possible that either Bill or Ivy had had an affair, broke up with this person, and this person couldn't accept that? Both Bill and Ivy were attractive people and had appeal.

As the report went on, Dr. White provided some general personality traits that would be common in the murderer IF this was indeed a crime committed by a serial killer:

1. Social withdrawal
2. Abnormal dependence on his mother
3. Hypochondria
4. Attention seeking behavior
5. Severe depression
6. General feeling of emptiness as to his future
7. Inability to take criticism
8. Failure to succeed in society
9. Inability to assert oneself

Numbers 1, 2, 6, 7, and 9 could be possible motives IF this crime was committed by a serial killer. It would be a start if he was going to pursue the serial killer theory. He would also need to see if there have been other couples in the area, the state or neighboring states who were murdered in the same manner and were cold cases or were believed to be committed by a serial killer. He seemed like he was trying to find a needle in a haystack. The challenge of catching a serial killer, however, did seem intriguing to him.

CHAPTER 19

Buford and Corbin moved from a conversation about their families to projects they wanted to get done around their houses to local and professional sports. Buford would look back frequently to see what Quinton Reed was doing. It appeared he was sleeping, but he could be faking. With prisoners you never could be sure.

"Oh, shit!" cried out Corbin.

Buford turned back to the front in time to see Corbin try to pull the steering wheel to the right to avoid an on-coming SUV. The vehicle with no headlights on, going the wrong direction on the highway, was practically on top of them. Before Corbin could do anything to avoid it, the speeding SUV hit them head on. The impact was so hard their transport vehicle went into a spin and careened down an embankment, rolling over once and landing back on its blown out front tires. The other vehicle had to have been traveling at 65 or 70 m.p.h. upon impact. Their airbags had deployed and a white powder was emitted, not to mention a pungent odor. The airbag was hot.

Buford felt like he had been hit in the face with a baseball bat. The seatbelt had retracted upon impact and had locked so tightly, he couldn't breathe. Blood was dripping into his eyes and down his face. His right wrist felt broken and his left leg was trapped under the smashed dash. He tried to work his leg out of there, but he was secured so tightly behind the seatbelt, he had no leverage. He tried unlocking the seatbelt but couldn't get the release button to work.

By the time the dust settled, so to speak, the car was dark and the engine was dead. He called out to Corbin who was slumped over the deflated, smoking airbag and the steering wheel. Corbin wasn't moving whatsoever. Buford called out again to Corbin but got no response.

How could this be happening? In all the years of transporting prisoners, nothing like this had ever happened. The windshield was so cracked, Buford couldn't see anything in front of him. Surely someone would soon come to their aid.

No doubt it was a drunk who hit them. Those guys usually always survived a wreck they caused when no one else walked away.

"Corbin? Corbin? Answer me! Are you okay, good buddy? Corbin!"

He tried to extend his left arm and shake Corbin to arouse him into consciousness. There was no sound or movement from Corbin who was immovable. Buford was afraid he might be dead, but he couldn't force himself to believe that. Just minutes ago they were discussing the Indians and the future season of the Cleveland Browns.

After what seemed to be at least five minutes, Buford managed to reach into the glove compartment and grab an emergency auto tool to help free him from the seatbelt. He took the seatbelt blade and cut the seatbelt in two. He felt quite light-headed and the amount of blood pouring down his face told him he must have incurred a pretty serious cut on his head. That actually seemed to be a minor concern for right now.

His left leg was still stuck under the dash, but he leaned over as far as he could to check Corbin. He was drenched in blood and was slumped forward. If he could get Corbin leaned back, he could study his face and check for a pulse. His left hand moved from the back of Corbin's neck down his back when he felt something hard protruding from it. To his horror, he discovered he was feeling a part of the steering wheel. Corbin had been impaled by it and was surely dead.

Hysteria overwhelmed him. The situation worsened when Buford realized that smoke was billowing from under the hood of the car, and he was still trapped inside. They all needed to get out of this vehicle before it exploded. The best scenario would be just a radiator leak from the collision, but so far things weren't going his way and he couldn't take a chance. Buford frantically tried to free his leg from the dash. His right hand was useless, so he used his left hand to try to force the dash upward thus allowing him to pull his leg out from under it. It took him three or four tries, but he finally freed his leg. He tried to open his passenger door and found that it was so smashed in, he couldn't open it from the inside. Luckily, he was able to take the emergency auto tool, using the glass hammer, and firmly tap the lower side window. The entire glass flew outward with the greatest of ease. So the tool works just as well as the advertisement said it would. One stroke of good luck.

For the first time, Buford thought of Reed. His primary concern had been for Corbin, his friend and cohort, but there was now no doubt about his fate. He hadn't survived. Buford's second responsibility was to the prisoner, but Buford instead decided to check for survivors of the SUV who hit them.

He literally had to climb out the small side window, coming out head first. Most of the glass had been broken out, but he still felt jagged edges cutting into his hands as he gripped the top and side of the window to pull himself out. Once he stood up, he realized how woozy he felt. He had superficial cuts on his hands and arms from broken glass and was bleeding, but he had, at least, survived this ordeal.

He quickly adjusted to the darkness and looked for the other vehicle involved, but there was nothing in sight. Perhaps it didn't follow them down the embankment and managed instead to stay on the road or careened off to the other side of the highway. Buford climbed the embankment. He saw pieces of metal, a hubcap, a fender, and broken glass but no SUV. He looked down the road and across the road in both directions.

"Damn, if this wasn't a hit and run! Whoever did this isn't going to get away with this."

He or she had to have so much damage to their vehicle, they could easily be found. The highway patrolman would collect so much evidence from their transport vehicle that the culprit would be found within a day or two, but perhaps not before he sobered up.

Buford heard a small pop and saw flames shooting out from under their hood. With little time to think, he rushed back to the car to check on Reed and try to get him out of there. He would then call for help. Had he been thinking clearly and not panicking, it wouldn't have been in that order.

CHAPTER 20

Buford pulled the car key from his side pant pocket and tried to unlock the back door of their vehicle. He couldn't see through the tinted windows. He figured there was a possibility that Reed could be seriously injured or even dead. Reed wouldn't have had a clear view of what was about to happen, so he couldn't have braced for it. All of the chains around his wrists, waist, and feet could have caused some significant injury. Not that Buford felt any sympathy whatsoever for him, but his job was to get Quinton to prison unharmed, and that, more than likely, wasn't going to happen.

Quinton had been sleeping when the impact occurred and was thrown around in the back seat. He hadn't seen it coming, but that may have worked to his advantage. He got a whiplash and hit his head on the armrest on the opposite side from where he had been sitting. It didn't take him long to get alert and assess what was happening when their vehicle rolled over. His head pounded into the window and split his forehead open.

He wasn't sure if this was some divinely orchestrated event intended just for him, but he realized this could be his one and only opportunity for escape. He certainly planned to take it.

Not knowing what to expect when he opened the back door, Buford was alert in case Quinton was able to try anything. The door had to be pulled and tugged on numerous times before it finally opened. When it finally opened, it got Buford off balance. He was feeling rather light headed anyway and was probably in shock.

He found Quinton's torso bent over his legs. He looked completely unconscious and was bleeding from his head. Bruising was already noticeable around his wrists.

Buford called out Reed's name but got no response. The smoke was billowing over the hood even more. Buford feared the car could explode any minute. Getting Reed out was crucial. He couldn't let him burn alive, no matter how mean he was, but Buford was going to do everything in his power—and he had actually hoped with Reed's assistance, though that was now pretty unlikely—to get Corbin's body out before the car went up in flames. That's the least he could do now for Corbin's family.

Buford leaned into the backseat to get his arms around Quinton in an effort to pull him out. He was quite sure his own wrist was broken, which left his right hand completely useless, and since he was right-handed, he would have to depend primarily on his left arm and hand to pull Quinton out of the car.

"Reed! Come on, Reed! Wake up! We've got to get out of this car now! It's going to go up in flames any minute!"

He tried to pat Quinton on the face to see if he could awaken him or get Quinton to assist himself out of the car. Reed seemed totally unresponsive. Quinton could have a broken neck for all he knew.

Buford put his left knee on to the backseat and thrust his body into the car to extend his left arm around Reed. Before Buford saw it coming, Quinton's chained arms came over Buford's head as quickly as a viper strike and Reed snapped his arms forward, snapping Buford's neck. He heard a loud snap and Buford gasped. Quinton took the chain and wrapped it as tightly as he could around Buford's neck. Stanley's spinal injuries were so serious by then that there was no strength left to sustain his defense and work the chain loose. Unmercifully, Reed squeezed the sides of the chain together in a choke hold so steadfastly that Buford had no room to wiggle and no leverage with which to struggle. With blood still pouring down his face, he could feel the breath of life leaving him. Reed's force on his throat and neck was unrelenting. The last thing Buford saw was the smirk on Quinton's face from the moonlight shining through the open car door.

Quinton crawled out of the car and pulled Stanley out as quickly as he could. He frantically rummaged through Buford's pockets until he found what he was looking for: the keys that would unlock the cuffs and belly chain and ultimately set him free.

CHAPTER 21

Quinton could hardly believe his good luck. He checked Daniels, the driver, and could easily determine he was dead. He then took the key out of the ignition and opened the trunk.

Bingo! Wasn't there a wonderful arsenal of weapons with plenty of ammunition! He was sure he could find use for those.

He saw the smoke billowing out from under the hood of the vehicle but saw no actual flames coming into the car. He tried to pull Daniels out of the car, but he was pinned in too tightly and there was no chance of Quinton pulling him out by himself.

Daniels seemed more his size, but Quinton wasn't able to unbutton his shirt and remove it. Then he realized he had been impaled. He took off his orange jumpsuit and threw it over Corbin's upper torso carelessly. He was going to have to put Stanley's uniform shirt on even though it would be too large.

Quinton returned to the far side of the car where Buford Stanley was lying on the ground. Quinton removed his shirt, trousers, socks, and shoes. The trousers were too long as Buford was about 2-3 inches taller than Quinton, and his feet were probably two sizes bigger than his. Somehow, Quinton would make it work.

Since he heard no ambulances, fire trucks, or cop cars, he realized these guys hadn't had time to radio for help. It was the best scenario he could ever have hoped for or imagined.

However, he needed to get out of this area as fast as he could. It wouldn't be long before the prison would realize the transport vehicle was late arriving and would be radioing them or sending the highway patrol out to find them. He couldn't get far on foot and with the bloodhounds, he would be found in no time.

Regardless of it being late at night, there would eventually be cars or trucks passing by either from the eastward or westward direction that he would have to commandeer. With an officer's uniform on, he could easily pull off a credible ruse.

He was now free of all the cuffs and chains and made his way up the embankment to the road. It was dark with no lights other than the moon's rays, but he could hear and feel his shoes crunching on shards of glass and pieces of metal from the accident. With that, Quinton planned his ruse but found he didn't have time to work through any details, for on the west side of the road he spotted car lights coming down the highway.

CHAPTER 22

Quinton quickly crossed over the median strip and waved his arms frantically as though in a panic. He knew the car's headlights had picked him up and that he could be seen by the driver. The car began to slow down and, fortunately, there were no other cars following.

The driver pulled the car over to the berm of the road and put on its bright lights. A man rolled down his window a fourth of the way. Quinton made sure his split forehead was visible.

"I'm so sorry, but I need help fast! The police and an ambulance are on the way. We've just been the victims of a hit and run driver. The impact sent us down the embankment over there. Do you have an emergency kit, sir? Please . . . my wife is trapped in the car and bleeding pretty badly! She was driving at the time, and I can't even get her out of the car to lay her down on the ground. Gauze, band-aids . . . anything to help stop the bleeding." He stopped in mid-sentence.

Quinton looked deeply concerned as he pled for his wife.

"Where is your car?"

"We rolled down the embankment! Do you see the glass and the other guy's grille there on the road? He came at us so fast. He didn't have his lights on and was driving on the wrong side of the road. I was sleeping . . . my wife didn't see him in time. Please . . . my wife. We need to stop her bleeding."

"You look pretty banged up yourself," said the driver. He did see remnants of the accident. *"You say the police are on their way?"*

"Yes, I hope they get here soon. We need an ambulance, but I can't stop her bleeding."

The man stepped out of the car and walked to his trunk to get his emergency kit and a large flashlight.

Meanwhile, Quinton crossed back over the highway and headed down the embankment to the transport vehicle. He knew the man would cross over and follow him in a second or two. And when he did, he would be ready for him. Quinton had the loaded gun he had found in the trunk cocked and was leaning over Daniels, blocking the man's view as he was standing at the top of the embankment holding a flashlight and assessing the situation, probably for his own personal safety. Buford Stanley's body was still on the ground on the other side of the car and out of view.

Quinton began to cry out.

"Ramona, hang in there. We're getting help. The ambulance will soon arrive. Please! Hang on, honey!"

The man started to walk down the embankment toward Quinton, holding his flashlight in his left hand and an emergency kit in the right hand. He was no more than three feet behind Quinton.

"Sir, let me have a look!"

"Okay," responded Quinton. He turned and put two bullets into the man's torso. Without hesitation, Quinton grabbed his flashlight, searched the man's pockets for his car keys, and needed to verified whether his Good Samaritan was dead. He was. Quinton took the man's wallet and quickly opened it up to check for I.D. and money. Charles Good. Well, he was rightly named, thought Quinton.

"Charles Good, meet Quinton Bad! Thanks for the wheels, pal"

Quinton grabbed all of the weapons and ammunition found in the trunk of the transport vehicle and climbed back up the embankment, crossed the highway once again, and got behind the wheel of his new Ford Fusion. The car had been heading west, which was exactly the direction Quinton wanted to go. He had some unfinished business in Akron.

CHAPTER 23

As Quinton headed westward on I-76, he had gone no further than a mile and a half when he saw a highway patrol car with its emergency lights flashing, a fire truck, and two ambulances. Flares were all over the road on the west side. Reed saw two mangled cars that had clearly collided head-on. The one car surely had to be the same one that had hit their vehicle and sent it careening down the embankment. Both cars were so mangled and broken apart, one would wonder how anyone could come out of either alive.

Fortunately for Reed, this would be such a distraction, he figured the transport vehicle he had been in might not be found for a day or two, along with the three dead men.

Traffic would be backing up soon and there would be quite a wait as it would take authorities quite a while to get the two cars towed and the highway cleaned up. Emergency crews would be so absorbed taking care of this horrific situation, they would never dream that an even deadlier situation lay up ahead another two miles or so.

Quinton maintained a normal speed to avoid drawing attention to himself. He would pick up his speed as soon as he felt it safe to do so.

An ambulance pulled away from the accident with its top warning lights on, traveling eastward. It had traveled no more than one mile when they heard a loud explosion up ahead and saw flames rising from down over the embankment. They increased their speed and arrived to see a car engulfed in fire.

The technicians radioed for help and both men ran down the embankment and rushed to the car. They spotted a driver trapped behind the steering wheel. The other EMT saw two bodies on the ground as he went to the other side of the car to check on possible passengers. He yelled for his buddy, and together they picked up a man and moved him away from the fiery car. They then went back to drag the second body away.

Upon closer inspection, they realized this incident entailed more than a car accident. At least one of these men had been shot. Both techs raced back to their ambulance, radioed for a fire truck as well as more police.

It was impossible to get the driver out of the car. The fire and smoke prevented them from trying to get to the poor guy, but he looked unsavable anyway.

Something really weird was going on tonight. Somehow they knew this night would be one to remember.

CHAPTER 24

Once they were able to radio in to the dispatchers what they saw and where, the fire truck was pulling up behind them. They pulled the ambulance back on the highway and headed for the nearest hospital. Other departments would need to be called in to assist.

For now, they had to get their victim to the hospital and would have to wait to hear what exactly was going on.

CHAPTER 25

As Quinton sped down the road, he pulled into a rest area and parked at the very far end away from the lights. He used the bathroom while no one was there and quickly returned to the Ford Fusion. He looked in the trunk to see what Charles Good had in it that might be useful to him. He found a blanket, tire iron, and a suitcase. In the glove compartment, he found a flashlight, the car's registration, some unmarked keys, and an Ohio map. In the front console he found change and a twenty dollar bill.

Quinton had put the guns from the transport vehicle on the front seat with him. He checked to see if they were loaded. They were. He studied them to make sure he knew how to use them. He knew quite a bit about weapons. His dad had quite a few of them in the house when he was a young boy and had taught him how to use them and to shoot. Even if the guns were styled differently, the concept for using them was pretty much the same.

Quinton went through Good's suitcase looking at his clothing. Lucky for him, Charles Good was almost the same size as he was. Quinton opted to change into Good's clothing in order to draw less attention to himself. Quinton first put on a tee shirt and then covered it with a light blue short sleeved dress shirt. It was a Van Heusen. Charlie had good taste! Then he put on a pair of his khaki Docker pants. Fortunately, they didn't have cuffs so the length looked pretty close to what he would have needed. He put on some of his dark brown GoldToe socks and then slipped his feet into Bass shoes, which were a perfect fit. He stuffed the other clothes from Daniel's and Stanley into the suitcase in case he would need them down the road.

Quinton knew it wasn't good to stay in one place too long. Can't let anyone get a hard, long look at you. Don't want to engage in conversation with anyone for fear of getting caught in a lie or arousing curiosity. He knew it wouldn't take long and his picture would be on every newscast and post office bulletin board—and everyone would be keeping their eye out for him.

Doug Conrad had been the source of all his problems and needed to pay for ruining his life. After he accomplished his mission and gave Conrad his recompense, he would flee across the border to Mexico and never return to the good ole U.S.A. He would settle down with a pretty seniorita . . . or *dos* . . . or *tres*. Quinton just laughed as he thought about that.

CHAPTER 26

Reed was sure Conrad and his children would be warned of his escape the minute it was discovered. They probably wouldn't imagine he would return to this area and take the risk of getting caught again!

If they thought it was feasible, they would probably hide the kids again—but not at Mitch Neubauer's home this time. Not having a clue where to find Taylor or Paul on their college campuses, Quinton decided to go after Conrad himself. That could give him enough satisfaction, even though he had wanted Conrad to suffer with each loss of his family members until he had no one left.

Quinton hoped to surprise Conrad before the authorities learned of the situation and could forewarn him. Therefore, he needed to get on the road and not tarry. The element of surprise is the key to a successful kill.

With his plan cemented in his memory, Quinton pulled on to I-76 once again and put the pedal to the metal.

CHAPTER 27

Officer Bryan Malone radioed in the license plate of the vehicle as the firemen were extinguishing the car. It was obvious the driver, at this point, could not be saved. An ME would need to be called to the scene as three bodies were found and one had two bullet holes through his torso.

Of course, no identification was found on either of the two bodies found on the ground. That in itself was suspicious.

"This vehicle is a transport vehicle for the state. Give us a few minutes and we should be able to provide more information."

Officer Malone had also called for more back up. As he left his vehicle, he walked down the embankment with his flashlight on. He had already blocked off the right lane of the highway with flares. The firemen had successfully extinguished the fire but the smoke was thick and acrid. The car would be too hot to even touch at this point.

As he scanned the surrounding grass, he saw the cuffs and belly chain lying together. The key was about a foot away. Bryan looked closely at the one body and saw the marks on the back of the man's neck, which he noticed, too, hung down abnormally. It looked like his neck was broken. Bryan pointed his flashlight into the wooded area but saw nothing. He had an eerie feeling. It appeared, at first, this was a car accident related to the one down the way, but something was very different.

Officer Malone heard the dispatcher and returned to his car.

"There were three men in the transport vehicle. Agents Corbin Daniels and Buford Stanley. They were transporting the infamous Quinton Reed to Ohio State Penitentiary to Death Row. He is the guy, as you probably know, who killed Cynthia Conrad," stated the dispatcher.

Bryan whistled as he realized the gravity of the situation.

"We have three bodies here, but the driver is burned beyond recognition. I can describe the two bodies I have on the ground, but things aren't making sense. Handcuffs and belly chains are sitting on the ground several feet away from where the victims were found. Why would the agent take off Reed's cuffs and chains?" asked Bryan.

The dispatcher listened carefully.

"Hold on, Officer Malone. I'll provide any description I can find on the parties. Am downloading now.

"Okay. Agent Corbin Daniels is a 33 year old. Dark brown hair, blue eyes, 5 feet, 11 inches tall, 175 lbs. Buford Stanley is a 35 yr. old African American, black hair, brown eyes, 6 feet1 inches tall, 165 lbs. I don't have specific information about Quinton Reed, but you probably remember what he looks like from seeing him on TV."

"We need to call OSP and see what time they were expecting Quinton Reed to arrive. Call the Akron Police Department and find out when they left the station and verify one more time who the transport agents were and when they were expected to arrive at OSP. If Reed has escaped, and I'm sensing that's the case, we need to get a BOLO and an APB out ASAP!"

CHAPTER 28

W ithin ten minutes Officer Malone was welcoming more officers to the scene and filling them in on what appeared to have happened when the ME and his crew arrived.

Special lights were set up to assist the medical examiner. Numerous photographs were taken not only of the wreckage, the position of the bodies and their visible wounds, but also of skid marks on the road, the broken glass splayed across the road that would inevitably help authorities re-enact this accident. If indeed that's what it was at first.

Observing the different color of car paint on the transport vehicle, and being aware of the other accident less than a mile down the same highway, it appeared the dead drunk driver had caused both accidents. The driver of the other car had been killed on impact also, but the front passenger and one strapped in the backseat were alive. They had sustained serious injuries and were being rushed to the hospital. Whether they could describe later what happened with any clarity may be asking too much, but authorities remained hopeful.

Bryan Malone returned to his car radio. The dispatcher confirmed the names of the transport agents, the time they left the Akron Police Department and the time they were scheduled to arrive at Ohio State Penitentiary.

The license plate matched the wrecked vehicle before them. It appeared one of the dead men fit the description of Buford Stanley, but the driver's body was burned beyond recognition. The other body lying on the ground with two bullet holes to his torso did not meet the description whatsoever of Quinton Reed. So their worst fear was coming to fruition. Quinton Reed was running loose, and this couldn't be good for anyone.

CHAPTER 29

No identity was found on the body lying on the ground. Who was he and where did he come from? One thing was certain: he was at the wrong place at the wrong time.

Because he was dressed in business attire, it appeared to Officer Malone that the man may have been traveling home from a business trip, came across the accident and stopped to help. Since there wasn't another car found on the side of the road, it was likely Quinton had confiscated it. If his theory was correct, they needed to identify this poor schmuck so they could identify his car and license plate and put a BOLO out on it. Of course, by then Quinton could have disposed of that car and stolen another and maybe at the expense of more lives. This guy was a *killing machine* and had to be stopped!

Officer Malone looked down at the smoldering car and the two dead bodies lying on the ground and one driver burned beyond recognition. Probably all three were good men with families—wives and children who loved them and now whose lives would be changed forever because of one evil man.

Bryan Malone had wanted to be a police officer since he was a kid. His uncle, whom he greatly admired, had been a policeman and had encouraged him to follow his dream. His uncle's stories of pursuing criminals and making the world a better place one day at a time had caught his attention and planted the seed since he was twelve or thirteen years old. He was a seeker of excitement and dreamed about being a hero. And, really, that's all Bryan ever wanted to do was be a policeman.

As the years went by, however, and he saw the depravity of man, he was sickened by it. Yes, he was making every effort to make it safer for the citizens of Ohio, but he found he wasn't really able to prevent crime at all. He cleaned up the mess *AFTER* all the devastation was complete. He had to fill out the crime reports in graphic detail to aid prosecutors in court. He had to appear in court oftentimes and be subjected to the interrogation of defense lawyers who would add a spin to the report or question his abilities or findings. They would try to degrade his professionalism, so all of the glamour he once had about the job as a teenager was gone. Tonight was the reality. There was no glamour in seeing family men killed by drunk drivers or convicted murderers who continued to hone their skills and were on the lam to kill again.

Families would soon be notified of this senseless tragedy. Tears would be shed over this night for a lifetime. Perhaps even the safety net and security would be ripped away from the children left behind. And guys like Quinton Reed walk away from their devastation without flinching or feeling for the survivors, much less their victims. And drunk drivers would continue to get behind the wheel of their cars and snuff out more lives.

Officer Malone could write a book about the many tragedies he had seen while on the job, but tonight was the worst. He wanted to believe in the goodness of man, but he was always seeing the other side of man. If he knew back then as a pre-teen what he knew now about the job and with the same level of maturity that he has now, he probably would have pursued a different career.

Bryan Malone would remain loyal to his career, but on nights like this one, he was reminded of a verse in the Bible that had always stuck with him: *"But every man is tempted, when he is drawn away of his own lust, and enticed. Then when lust hath conceived, it bringeth forth sin and sin, when it is finished, bringeth forth death."*

As he looked down at the scene, he saw the bodies being placed in body bags. Very soon they would be on their way to the county morgue to undergo an autopsy.

Probably the last place they would have imagined themselves going tonight, thought Bryan.

With that, he turned and returned to his cruiser.

CHAPTER 30

Sgt. Dennis Parker was awakened at 12:20 a.m. by the phone ringing. His children were already out of the nest, so usually when the phone rang at this hour, it was the department with bad news. It also usually meant he would have to return to the department immediately.

"Dennis Parker here."

"Sergeant. This is Officer Trent. We just got word that Quinton Reed escaped from his transport vehicle on the way to OSP. Right now his location is unknown. An APB has been released, but we thought you should know."

"That bastard! How could this have happened?"

"From what we know their vehicle was hit head-on by a hit and run drunk driver. The transport was found down a small embankment, on fire. A mile away the drunk had hit another vehicle, killing himself, the driver of that car, and injuring two other passengers. But when the transport vehicle was finally discovered, three dead bodies were found—none of these was Reed. The vehicle had caught on fire and one body, the driver, was burned beyond recognition. We don't think too much time had lapsed before the vehicle was found. One of the bodies, I was told, took two shots to the belly. There were no witnesses."

"How does Reed get so damn lucky? What were the odds of that happening? Are we sure this wasn't more than a stroke of good luck for him? Could it have been an escape plan or someone was working in collusion with Reed?"

"The patrolmen were pretty certain at this point that it started as an innocent accident. Of course, their investigation hasn't been completed."

"Has Doug Conrad been notified yet?"

"No."

"I'll call him. I think we may need to get the SWAT team out to his house for protection and find his kids and put them in protective custody until Reed is found. We can't take any chances with this character. How much more havoc can Reed put this one family through? Let me make a few calls, and I'll head back to the department. Be there in about a half hour. Thanks, Officer Trent."

Sgt. Parker's wife was wide awake, listening to the phone conversation. She was able to figure out from his side of the conversation what had happened. Her husband had been so troubled and touched by this case more than any other he had been involved in during their marriage, and now she could see the strain on his face again.

Sgt. Parker hurried out of bed and went into the kitchen and looked up Doug Conrad's phone number. As the phone was ringing the Conrad home, Dennis could only imagine how Doug was going to react. He himself couldn't believe this was happening.

After four rings, he heard Doug's voice.

"Conrad's residence. This can't be good news at this time of the night. What's going on, Sgt. Parker?" Doug asked.

Obviously, Doug had caller I.D. This, in part, made it easier for him to cut to the chase.

"Yes, Doug. I've got bad news, for sure. I just received a call saying Quinton Reed escaped from the transport vehicle while on his way to OSP."

He heard Doug gasp quietly.

"I doubt seriously that he would come after you or the kids, but we aren't taking any chances. You need to get hold of your kids immediately and have them drive to the nearest police station for protective custody. I'm going to get a small SWAT team positioned around your house, Doug. Surely he wouldn't be stupid enough to come after you, but in the event

that he is, we'll be waiting for him. He's armed , Doug, so be cautious and alert. Let Mitch know also. I'll be in touch with you shortly."

"I'll call my kids and Mitch right now, Dennis."

"I'm going to head for the station to coordinate the SWAT team. You may not see us, Doug, but we will be in place, watching your house closely. No heroics, buddy. Keep your alarm system and cell phone on."

CHAPTER 31

D onna Gifford was watching a late night movie on TV when there was breaking news about Quinton Reed's escape. Few facts were given but clearly Reed's location was unknown.

Donna got on the phone and called Mitch Neubauer, figuring Doug had already been notified of the situation. Mitch had already learned of Reed's escape through Doug and assured her that he and Elaine would be watchful and alert. However, he expressed concern for Doug and the kids. In the course of the conversation, he suggested that she and Barnabus go over to Doug's house as extra protection.

"You'll have to force your way in by being insistent, Donna. Doug tries to protect everyone else, but right now my gut tells me if Reed doesn't try to leave the country, he will head straight to the Conrad house and attempt to kill Doug. The guy is crazy! Doug needs your help but will never ask for it."

After hanging up the phone, Donna called Barnabus and updated him on Quinton Reed's escape and the jeopardy Doug could be in. Barnabus volunteered to pick Donna up at her mother's house where she was temporarily staying and both drive to Doug's home in Green.

Barnabus grabbed his loaded gun and put extra ammunition into his backpack. While Donna waited for Barnabus to arrive, she, too, loaded her SIG SAUER with its built-in laser and put it into her shoulder holster under her blue blazer. She loaded her purse with extra ammunition.

Barnabus had to have broken all speed limits to have arrived at her house ten minutes after talking to her by phone. He was dressed casually but neatly—all in black. She couldn't help but notice how muscular he was. He obviously worked out on a regular basis. His casual shirt accented his broad shoulders and chest, bulging biceps and trim belly. He looked military.

Ten minutes later Barnabus parked his black 2011 MX-5 Miata in a cul-de-sac, five houses down from Conrad's home. He and Donna checked out their surroundings—all the driveways, unlit and lit houses, trees and bushes before stepping out of the car. With quick strides, they walked to Doug's front door which suddenly opened before they could ring the doorbell. Mitch had alerted Doug of their coming and purpose. Doug had spoken to Paul and Taylor and was convinced both were safe and were being protected at local police stations that were aware of the situation.

Doug updated Donna and Barnabus on Sgt. Parker's plan. Doug was to keep all of his house lights off with the exception of night lights. His security system was put back on after Donna and Barnabus arrived. Some of his drapes were partially drawn, restricting a view either inside or out.

Dr. Brandon White had been called. He had been the APD's criminal profiler for Quinton Reed. It was his belief that Reed could very well return to Conrad's house to finish his job.

Two SWAT team members were in place: one in Lucy and John Roger's home across the street and one outside, hidden in the trees of Conrad's backyard.

Barnabus was to remain on the main floor with Doug, watching out the various windows for suspicious movement or a dim light as well as listening for any unusual sounds. Donna was to do the same upstairs. In the likely event that Reed did show up tonight, the main floor would most likely see the action. However, Reed made his appearance on the second floor when he broke into Mitch's home, so no one was minimizing the importance of keeping vigil upstairs. Criminals are prone to repeat their habits.

Everyone was hoping that Reed would be audacious and arrogant enough to show up. Things could go terribly wrong for Reed this time.

CHAPTER 32

When Doug got the call from Sgt. Parker that Quinton had escaped, he felt like a rug had been pulled out from under him. When was this ordeal with Quinton Reed ever going to end? Fear welled up inside of him, a fear especially for the safety of his kids. Could Reed's escape send his kids over the edge? Their emotional wounds were still fresh. Paul and Taylor had just recently completed counseling because of their mom's murder and Reed's assault on them at Mitch Neubauer's house. This could certainly be a setback in their healing process—more so for Taylor than Paul. Until Reed was captured and put away, their family could never feel safe again.

Very few times in Doug's life had he been truly afraid. While working on patrol as a police officer, he had pulled his gun out of its holster a myriad of times, ready to fire at an assailant, but, fortunately, he never once had to fire it at anyone. When he was most afraid, however, was when something happened to his family.

He remembered when Paul was born. Cynthia had been healthy throughout her entire pregnancy, and then within minutes while in labor at Akron General Medical Center, things started deteriorating. Her blood pressure became dangerously elevated. Every time her uterus contracted, the baby's heart rate went down. Dr. Mitchell suspected the baby's umbilical cord was wrapped around his neck and Cynthia's desire for a natural birth fell by the wayside. She was rushed into the operating room for a caesarian. He remembered watching those double doors close in front of him, not knowing if Cynthia or the baby would live.

Then he remembered the time when Taylor was four years old and their puppy got out of the house and ran into the street. Taylor, in her childlike faith, ran after it without even looking and was almost hit by a car. Both she and the puppy had a happy ending, but not all bad occurrences end happily, as he so well knew.

Cynthia had been killed by the hands of this madman and now he and his family could be in jeopardy by Reed once again. Well, Doug had had enough and was ready to bring this problem to a conclusion once and for all.

Ever the professional detective, Doug felt an adrenaline rush and was on high alert, watching and waiting for a potential confrontation with his night visitor—his greatest enemy. But Doug also knew that he was so emotionally distraught, worrying about the personal safety of his kids, that he could easily be distracted and make an error in judgment or a mistake. So, he was very receptive to having Donna and Barnabus in his home to be watchful as well. If Reed was going to make a move to kill him, he would need to do it quickly before more details were known about what vehicle he was using or before law enforcers caught him.

This also gave Doug the opportunity to observe the operations and tactics of his two newest employees. He was already impressed that they had volunteered to come to his aid. It wasn't something he expected at all, but clearly they were team players and he greatly appreciated their presence and professionalism. Just knowing they were in the house with him helped him to calm down considerably.

Doug had talked to both Paul and Taylor and officers at each one of their police stations and felt assured they would be safe. But then he remembered when they were home, under the watchful eye of a police officer, when both kids sneaked out of the house undetected. He hoped and prayed they had both learned their lesson from those acts of disobedience and would never repeat them under these similar circumstances.

CHAPTER 33

Taylor believed she was living deja vu all over again. She was directed by Sgt. Parker and her dad to stay at this small police station under the supervision and safety of the local Kent police. How long she was to simply sit in their small lobby no one said. It was temporary, she knew, but if Quinton Reed didn't get found within several hours, her dad was going to arrange for her to stay somewhere else where she would be more comfortable but her location would be unknown.

Kent was a small college town and officers weren't plentiful. No one was told to sit and hold her hand. An officer was present at the station , so there was a safety net for her.

However, as she sat there idly, she contemplated her situation and didn't like it. When Kevin Reed had kidnapped her, he took her to West Virginia to be under his dad's control. But when she was delivered to the location in the woods, she later learned that her mother was in those woods running for her life and, ultimately, murdered there. Taylor, knowing that something was wrong, ran for help that came too late. Retrospectively, had she stayed—or even run into the woods, Quinton Reed might have gotten distracted long enough for her mom to have gotten away.

And, now, her dad's life was probably in jeopardy, and what was *she* doing? Cowering in a police station, doing nothing to help him. At least if she was home with her father, together they could watch out for one another. If anything happened to her dad, she couldn't live with herself. If Dad was killed, she didn't want to live either.

Self-induced panic erupted inside her. This was all too crazy! This Reed guy was controlling everyone and had killed too many people already. When was he going to be stopped? Everyone seemed to be puppets, marching to his whims. Taylor didn't want to live in fear anymore. Hadn't her counselor taught her that she owned her own emotions and life and that she needed to take them back? Well, she planned to do just that!

The officer's back was turned to her. He appeared to be typing reports or something on the computer. He had a huge pile of papers in front of him that he seemed to be working on. He appeared engrossed and task-oriented.

Quietly, she decided to walk out of the station leaving some of her school books and things there so that when he did look up, the officer would simply think she had stepped into the restroom for awhile.

Taylor stepped out of the station without making a sound and got into her Century Buick, which was parked a half block from the station. She looked around cautiously and started the car. As soon as she put the car in drive, all doors locked, and she was on her way home to Green. From Kent it would take about 25 minutes even though it was late and there'd be no traffic problems.

She knew her dad would be upset with her, but he would get over it. Besides, he could protect her and during this crisis, she preferred being home.

CHAPTER 34

The two member SWAT team was set up merely on a hunch. When Dr. Brandon White predicted a criminal's potential actions and thought processes, he was usually right. While it sounded like a bizarre plan for Reed to show up at the Conrad home, Reed himself was a totally bizarre and unpredictable kind of guy. He was definitely a risk taker. However, the Summit County Sheriff's office felt that two team members would be sufficient. In the event that Reed didn't show up, the city hadn't put that much money into the evening.

Russell Gates, armed with an AK-47, was positioned in Lucy and John Roger's upstairs bedroom, with their permission, of course. There he could have a perfect frontal view of the Conrad home. He could see the entire driveway, the front door and even see in a few windows where the shades weren't down or the drapes drawn completely closed. It would seem more natural that way and would look like Conrad wasn't expecting anyone.

Gates and his partner, Ralph Holton, were armed with the Cobra ear boom headsets strapped to their helmets. Ralph, wearing his black outfit with Kevlar panels and his tactical goggles, was positioned in a tree in the woods behind Conrad's home. There he had a perfect view of the back and sides of Doug's home. It would be almost impossible to be spotted in the woods by a civilian.

Doug Conrad and two of his detectives inside the home were armed, and the Summit County deputies were alerted to the situation and ready to assist if needed. At the present time, however, they had strict instructions to have no involvement and show no presence near the Conrad home. If Reed was coming after Conrad, he would do it as quickly as possible, especially if he believed no one was yet aware of his escape. The element of surprise was powerful but, hopefully, it would backfire on Reed. The last thing their superiors had admonished them about concerning Reed was not to underestimate him. He was crafty and no one was certain at this point what weapons he was in possession of or what he was wearing. One thing was certain: when Reed fired a gun, he didn't miss. That in itself didn't alarm the sharpshooters who felt Reed was no match in skill to their training and their weaponry, but it was important to know who they were dealing with and his psychological frame of mind.

Tonight Reed would be more alert than ever, but there were five trained police officers equally alert, and if he showed up, they would know it quickly and be able to inform one another of his location and every move.

CHAPTER 35

A Summit County deputy in an unmarked car drove through Doug Conrad's neighborhood in an effort to spot any cars of suspicion without drawing attention to himself. Interestingly enough, he spotted a car three blocks away from Conrad's home parked in a cul-de-sac with a Pennsylvania license plate. He called it in to the dispatcher and learned the car belonged to Charles Good who lived in New Castle, Pennsylvania. He had no criminal record and no points on his license plate. If Good was visiting someone on that street, why wouldn't he have been parked in that person's driveway? Curious, the deputy decided to have the dispatcher call the New Castle police to find out more information on Good. What he found out next was a shock to him and, perhaps, the break they were looking for.

One of the dead bodies found by the side of I-80 east had a cell phone. The authorities took it and called a few of the numbers in it only to find out that the owner of the cell phone was Charles Good. They were able to call his wife from that phone and find out from Mrs. Good where her husband was. He was on his way to North Canton, Ohio to The Timken Company for business.

Now they had the identification of the third body found.

"Was your husband driving a business vehicle, Mrs. Good?"

"No, this time he was driving his own personal car . . . his Ford Fusion."

Within a few minutes, the SWAT team was made aware of the suspicious car, its location, and the significance to their situation. Reed was in the vicinity.

CHAPTER 36

Snuggles, Conrad's Shih-tzu, sniffed Barnabus Johnson who was sitting on the floor beside the living room picture window. She looked up at him begging for a belly rub. Barnabus, nicknamed Zap by his army buddies, leaned forward and petted Snuggles on the head and rubbed her ears gently. It was the dog's way of getting acquainted with this new guest in the home.

As if on cue, she moved toward the steps and quickly ascended the stairs. All of the doors leading to the bedrooms and bath were left open. Snuggles quickly found their second visitor kneeling beside a bedroom window. Without talking to the dog, which would have occurred under normal circumstances, Donna refused to be distracted from her purpose for being there. Snuggles gently nudged against Gifford, making sure she knew she was there, but when she received no gratification, she made her way back downstairs.

Even Doug paid little attention to Snuggles. He moved quietly from room to room, occasionally peeking out a window unobtrusively. Doug really wanted the dog out of their way and safe from any harm, but he knew if he locked her in the basement, she would bark her head off. After she got used to Barnabus and Donna, she would probably go find her dog pillow beside Doug's La-Z-boy chair in the family room, lie down, and fall asleep.

Since Cynthia was gone, Snuggles seldom left Doug's side when he was home. The two had bonded to one another in an inexplicable way after their mutual loss. Snuggles was a very docile, undemanding, and lovable dog. It was so easy to love her. She gave back much more than she got.

Ten minutes later Snuggles left her pillow and started whining. Her ears had perked up and she stood in an alert position. She walked to the front door and stood there as though she wanted out. There was no way Doug was going to open the door and let Snuggles out. He wondered if maybe it would be better to simply lock her in the basement, but if she barked and Reed came to the door, Reed would surmise that Doug couldn't possibly sleep through that noise.

Snuggles was clearly restless and kept staring at the front door. She sat on her hind legs in alert mode and began woofing softly. Her head tilted as she responded to an inaudible sound. Then she started pacing back and forth along the front wall. Both Barnabus and Doug picked up on it and sensed that someone was out there—perhaps even on the other side of the door. Was it possible that Reed was already here?

Barnabus whispered into his borrowed ear boom headset, informing Gates and Holton of the family pet's instincts. A dog's hearing and awareness were so much better than any human, it would be remiss to ignore it.

Now everyone was on high alert and the adrenaline was coursing through their veins.

Just then a car came barreling down the road with its lights on. There was nothing inconspicuous about this car. It was too dark at first to see the license plate or the make of the car. There were no street lights so there was little chance of identifying the car or driver even with tactical goggles on until it got a little closer. The car was starting to slow down and quickly made a turn into Conrad's driveway.

Gates was able to read the license plate and read it off to the team and to a dispatcher. Seconds later Doug realized the number Gates had just read off.

"Oh, my God, that's Taylor's car! How could this be? She was supposed to be at the police station under full protection."

Just then Taylor abruptly stopped the car at the head of the driveway and turned the car off. For just a few seconds she studied their house. Except for a few night lights on, the house was dark. How could this be? Surely her dad wouldn't be sleeping, knowing that Quinton Reed was on the loose. He would be up and alert, waiting for Reed. What if Reed had already arrived and killed her dad? Maybe her dad was lying on the floor inside the house bleeding to death? Maybe Reed abducted her dad like he did her mom and had already taken him to a secondary location. Things just didn't look right. She was gripped with fear. She pulled her cell phone out of her purse, jumped out of the car and began dialing her house phone while walking toward the front door. Then she thought it might just be quicker if she yelled for her dad. He could meet her at the door to let her in.

Vacillating, she walked rapidly down the driveway and actually decided to take a shortcut across the front yard to reach the front door more quickly. She reached into her purse for her house key only to realize she hadn't brought it with her and would need to ring the doorbell after all.

While multi-tasking and being distracted, she didn't notice someone stepping out from behind the arborvitae tree in the front of the house.

Russell Gates saw his worst nightmare playing out in front of him as he realized just who the man was.

"Reed's stepping toward Taylor with a weapon in his hand, but I can't get a clear shot at him. Taylor's in the way!" Gates shouted.

Just then Doug opened the front door with no weapon visible and screamed.

"Get down, Taylor! Get down!"

Doug ran toward Taylor and Reed who had a gun pointed directly at Taylor's chest.

"No, Reed! It's me you want! Here I am. Take me!"

Reed turned toward the front door to see Doug running toward him with no weapon in hand. Quinton knew he could shoot both Doug and Taylor in mega-seconds. Tonight was going to be a bonanza for him—two Conrads in one night!

Ralph Holton assessed his surroundings before climbing down from the tree. He sprinted for the front yard, knowing he couldn't get there on time.

Donna Gifford, who was looking out the upstairs window, realized the dilemma for Gates, and before Doug took his next step forward, she fired her SIG SAUER P220 straight at Reed whose finger was ready to press down on the weapon's trigger that was aimed straight at Doug.

Taylor was standing less than two feet from Reed and realized the danger she and her dad were both in.

The next second blood squirted all over Taylor. Reed fell backward on her as the gunfire resounded. There was a short gasp.

It was a second of horror and then Taylor and Reed collapsed into darkness.

CHAPTER 37

Barnabus Johnson ran out of the house toward Doug Conrad and the two bodies lying on the ground. Doug Conrad was a private detective and a former cop, but at the present time he was a distraught father and a victim himself.

Donna Gifford continued to stare out the window in disbelief. There was no way she could have hit Taylor. No way at all, and yet Taylor had blood all over her and was completely unconscious. Donna holstered her gun and rushed downstairs.

Doug was crying, shaking, and leaning over Taylor, calling out her name. Barnabus side-stepped Doug, putting his hand on Doug's shoulder.

"Step aside, Doug. Let me check her."

While it was dark and Taylor was dressed in jeans and a dark top lying in the grass, Barnabus was pretty sure he knew Taylor's condition.

Meanwhile Gates made his way out of the Rogers' home and watched as Holton checked Reed's vitals and determined he was dead. Holton called the Summit County Sheriff requesting an ME and paramedics to the Conrad residence in Green.

Barnabus carefully lifted Taylor into his arms and gently carried her into the Conrad house.

"Doug, she's fine. She's going to be just fine! She's simply fainted from total fear. I saw this in Iraq all the time. Taylor's been through a lot. I think it's going to be finally over for your family."

Barnabus laid her on the couch and Donna, with a sigh of relief, brought a cool cloth to put on her brow. Doug was standing over the couch watching everything that was being done for Taylor.

"Are you okay, Doug?" asked Donna.

"It all happened so fast! She could have been killed!"

Snuggles jumped up on the couch and began to lick Taylor's face. Taylor's eyes started to open and she felt Snuggles's wet tongue on her cheek. For a moment, Taylor seemed a bit confused until reality hit her. When she looked up and saw all the adults standing over her, she was a bit overwhelmed.

"Dad! Please, tell me it's all over! Are you all right?"

"I'm fine, Taylor! Are you okay?"

"Is he dead, Dad? Is Quinton Reed dead?"

Doug looked up at Gates and Holton who nodded assent.

"Yes, Taylor, he's dead. Our nightmare has finally ended."

Taylor sobbed and her dad came around to her side and held her, getting much of Reed's blood all over him, but Conrad didn't care. His daughter needed comforting, and he needed her comfort. Their drama began in this house six months ago, and, ironically, it finally ended at this house.

The paramedics arrived and walked over to the couch to examine Taylor. While they were busy looking Taylor over, Doug stepped inside the kitchen and called Paul on his cell phone. He wanted his son to hear the story from him first before hearing it from the press or a secondary source.

Tears streamed down Doug's face as he shared the night's events. He hadn't recalled ever crying like this until Reed entered their lives and took Cynthia away from them. He could hear Paul crying on the other end too. Both men were shook up but relieved that tonight's events had ended with a fitting ending. Quinton Reed would never hurt another soul again. Clearly his soul was abscessed.

Even though Doug had assured Paul that he and Taylor were fine, Paul insisted on coming home and seeing for himself. It was a busy time at school, but one day wouldn't hurt. He needed to be with his family.

"I love you, son, and will be looking forward to seeing you tomorrow."

"I love you too, Dad. Get some rest, if you can. Tell Taylor I love her."

CHAPTER 38

Taylor was still responding to the paramedics' questions as they hovered over her. She seemed to be okay at the moment, so Doug decided to step out onto his front yard.

Quinton was lying on the ground. Since the ME hadn't arrived yet, everyone had to be careful not to contaminate any evidence around his body. Conrad looked up and saw Donna Gifford in the back of the squad car, unsure why she was there. She looked out the window and their eyes met. She had such a sweet, concerned look on her face and, yet, seemed so calm.

Doug stood several feet away from Reed and looked down at his bloody body. His face, surprisingly, seemed placid. So many emotions coursed through Doug's mind regarding the man who had attempted to wipe out his entire family.

Doug felt no sympathy for Reed. You live by the sword, you die by the sword, and so it was with Reed. Doug had always been taught that you live your life in such a way that your days may be prolonged. In fact, when he was a kid in vacation Bible school, they had to memorize Proverbs 10:27: *The fear of the Lord prolongeth days, but the years of the wicked shall be shortened.*

The one thing that did sadden Doug about Reed was that he never left a good legacy for his own family. He brought reproach upon the family name for his three sons. Reed had three sons who needed him, and now his memory would only bring them a heavy heart. He knew Ramona could now rest more peacefully and feel safe again, but he also knew she would have a kaleidoscope of mixed emotions and memories. Hopefully, she and the boys shared a few good ones of Quinton somewhere in their past.

You don't watch people die violently and feel gallant about it, even if that person murdered your wife. Was there anyone in this world who had loved Quinton and would miss him? No one had shown up on his behalf in court to offer mitigating circumstances for saving Reed from the death penalty, and yet he understood Reed's mother was still alive and had been notified.

Was Reed ever loved and cared for properly in his youth? Reed's ex-wife had mentioned that his parents were divorced when Reed was a fairly young boy. His father tried to make himself accessible to his son, but the mother lied about his being physically and emotionally abusive, and so the father eventually was denied visitation rights and walked away from Quinton's life altogether.

Doug was so proud of his kids. He and Cynthia loved each other first and foremost, and then they loved and nurtured Paul and Taylor as much as any parent could. That reminded him of Proverbs 22:6: *Train up a child in the way he should go, and when he is old, he will not depart from it.* It was Biblical advice that worked in his home. He couldn't be more proud of the direction both Paul and Taylor were taking in their lives. Too bad Quinton didn't have the advantage of the same upbringing. The outcome, in all probability, would have been better for Quinton, and Cynthia would be alive today.

He had actually stepped out of the house to seek closure and find satisfaction in seeing Quinton's dead body, but his reaction was the opposite. He felt total and complete sadness. All of the grief Quinton had showered on so many people was preventable. Nobody won.

Doug turned to walk back into the house when he looked up and saw Donna still in the backseat of the squad car. He started to walk over to it when one of the SWAT team members, Russ Gates, intercepted him.

"Mr. Conrad, I know this has been a rough and scary night for you and your daughter, but we're happy that only the perpetrator was hurt."

"Yes, I thank God for that too. Thanks so much for being here and for all you did."

"You're welcome. Holton and I were both thankful your two detectives were here tonight. The outcome might have been different."

"What do you mean?"

Russ Gates gave Conrad an inquisitive look and then realized that since everything happened so quickly and Conrad was so personally involved in the situation, he wasn't able to see how the shooting played out.

"Why, Taylor's body blocked my sight on Reed so I wasn't able to take the shot without risking injury to Taylor. Your detective . . . Donna Gifford . . . took the lethal shot from the upper bedroom window that saved Taylor's life. She was a quick reactor. You could tell she had been on a SWAT team herself."

CHAPTER 39

Doug had no idea Donna was the one who shot and killed Quinton. He was so grateful both of his new employees saw the need, without even asking, to come help him. It clinched for him the quality of these two new employees. He would be forever grateful to them. Their presence alone gave him comfort. They certainly worked as a team tonight, and he felt overwhelmed.

Doug walked over to the squad car and knowing the back door was locked, he asked an officer if he could join Mrs. Gifford in the backseat for several minutes. Under the circumstances, no one would deny Doug Conrad anything.

The door was opened and Doug crawled in beside Donna. Doug started to get choked up.

"Are . . . are you okay, Donna?"

"I'm fine, Doug. It's never easy taking the life of anyone, but just so you know . . . Reed wasn't my first."

"You saved . . . my . . . daughter tonight. I didn't know it was you until a few minutes ago. How do I thank you enough?"

"No need to, Doug. It became a part of our job tonight. Thankfully, we all had the headsets on that allowed me in time to know Gates couldn't take the shot. I did only what I had to do. Now you had better get back to your daughter. I'm fine. I'll be going to the police station to complete the report."

"Take tomorrow off, Donna. I'll touch base with you sometime in the afternoon."

Tears welled up again in Doug's eyes, and he took her left hand that was resting on the seat and brought it up to his lips for a gentle, affectionate kiss.

"Thank you," he whispered as tears streamed down his face.

Donna watched him as he walked toward his front door. He was emotionally spent. Doug was a strong, masculine type of guy, but the threat on his family had taken its toll on him. She knew that after tonight, the healing process could begin.

CHAPTER 40

Donna Gifford was sitting at her desk, reading a police report and a few newspaper articles about Quinton Reed's escape on Interstate 80 East and the events of that evening. Three men died that night, two at the cruel hands of Reed, making him the murderer of five people in all. Previously, he had nearly killed Mitch and Elaine Neubauer, and within seconds would have killed Doug and Taylor Conrad had she not shot him to death. He was a pretty cruel and heartless guy.

Killing people was the last thing Donna ever wanted to do. She actually turned to this career to help people and make society safer. Killing Reed did make society a lot safer, so while she didn't rejoice in having to kill him, neither did she feel remorse or guilt over it. She saved two good, productive people from being slain that night, and spared them from a life of continued fear and stress. She knew Reed had changed Doug Conrad's life forever, but in time, he would heal and move on as would his children.

Meanwhile her thoughts needed to return to the case they were working on before Reed had taken center stage. She went back seventeen years into Ivy Chandler's journal when she first dated and married Bill and became a stepmother to Andrew.

Ivy had married late in life and she and Bill had together made the decision to not have children. Bill had Andy and Ivy now had a stepson she could love and be devoted to. It was clear from her writings that she was excited about having a stepson. Being a teacher, she loved kids and had always wanted to marry and have at least two of her own. Unlike many of her peers, she believed in marriage first and then having children, so in this way she felt God blessed her with a child to love after all.

Bill's divorce had been anything but amicable. He had been devastated when he finally learned of the deception and betrayal—not only by his wife but his good friend and neighbor. Nevertheless, he rose above the emotional pain and was a gentleman throughout the divorce proceedings and the whole ugly mess. So in their marriage counseling sessions, Ivy had been warned that problems between Rita and Bill would get even worse *after* they were married. Ivy didn't understand the reasoning for the escalation since Rita had been the one to leave Bill for a family friend. Rita had actually married the guy and seemed to be happily married. Why would she resent Bill for starting his life over and finding happiness?

Bill had been divorced for over a year when he and Ivy met. They were introduced while at a charity function and dated three years before marrying. That gave Ivy the opportunity to know what she was getting into. She came to love Bill's family and had built a very warm and loving relationship with little Andy.

Ivy's family had accepted Bill and Andy with open arms, so there didn't seem to be big concerns about his previous failed marriage. Bill and Ivy were committed to each other first and committed to Andy secondly. Both were also committed to keeping their marriage vows.

Donna paused to think about this sweet couple and what could have gone so wrong in their lives to end by murder. It was so unfair. To let someone get away with their deaths would be a travesty of justice. It couldn't go unsolved. It just couldn't.

CHAPTER 41

Pastor Jim Pascoe and his wife Holly invited Doug, Paul, and Taylor over for dinner before the children returned to their respective colleges to complete the final weeks of school.

The relationship between Jim and Doug went much deeper than pastor and parishioner. They were close friends, had been for years. Jim had been the person Doug turned to most when Cynthia was missing. He was comforter and confidant. Jim and Holly loved Paul and Taylor and counseled them throughout the entire ordeal. And, now, they were in Pascoes warm and inviting home discussing the events of the previous day and Reed's death over a delicious meal Holly had prepared for them.

No one could calm hearts and fears like Jim and Holly. They were so grounded in their faith and seemed to know how to deal with the moments of diversity that make most mortals doubt whether a loving God could really put them through such heinous experiences.

The Conrad family had been dealt a bad hand this past year. That was for sure. They had to go through more tragedy than most people go through in their lifetime. Paul and Taylor had openly expressed their feelings about Quinton Reed and the trauma he had put the entire family through as they sat around the dinner table. The adults gave them as much time to verbalize as they needed. Sometimes their anger came through. Then tears would stream down their face. Their spirit had been broken at the realization that their mom was never coming back again.

It was the most poignant realization. They felt such loss. They were exasperated by the indelible memory of Reed's trial and the defense lawyers making excuses for Reed's behavior.

It was insightful to Doug as he listened to his children and watched their facial expressions. As he listened to his children processing the collateral damage to themselves and their dad, he also witnessed an inner strength, a determination, a will to overcome it and not allow Reed the final victory—a claim on their future happiness and sense of safety. It was a page turner for his kids.

The five moved from the dining room to the Pascoes family room. There was an evening chill so Jim turned the gas fireplace on. They sat in a close circle—a room deliberately set up for tonight's company. It seemed divinely orchestrated to Doug. Jim Pascoe asked each one to lift up a prayer to God regarding their emotional and spiritual needs and to express their honest feelings toward God.

Doug wasn't sure what to expect from Paul or Taylor, but he was amazed—perhaps shocked—by the depth of their trust in God. He would never forget one particular comment spoken by Paul . . ."*If I walked with no sorrow and lived with no loss, Lord, would my soul seek your sweet solace at the foot of the cross?*"

And then as Taylor prayed, her comment that struck him was, "*If I never felt pain would I search for your hand to help and sustain?*"

How profound coming from two kids in their late teens and early twenties.

Then Holly stepped over to the baby grand piano and began playing a familiar hymn to everyone sitting in the room. It was so sweet and solemn. Jim proceeded to remind them of the history of this sweet and meaningful hymn written by Horatio Spafford in 1873:

"*This hymn was actually written after two major traumas in Spafford's life. In the Great Chicago Fire in 1871, Spafford, a very wealthy businessman, was ruined financially. Shortly after, while crossing the Atlantic, all four of his daughters died in a collision with another ship. Only Spafford's wife survived. Several weeks later as Spafford's own ship*

passed near the spot where his daughters died, the Holy Spirit inspired
him to write these words which speak of eternal hope that all believers
have, no matter what pain and grief befall them on earth:

When peace like a river attendeth my way,
When sorrows like sea billows roll,
Whatever my lot, Thou has taught me to say,
It is well, it is well, with my soul.

But, Lord, tis for Thee, for Thy coming we wait,
The sky, not the grave, is our goal;
Oh trump of the angel! Oh voice of the Lord!
Blessed hope, blessed rest of my soul!

And Lord, haste the day when my faith shall be sight,
The clouds be rolled back as a scroll,
The trump shall resound, and the Lord shall descend,
Even so, it is well with my soul!

It is well, it is well,
With my soul,
It is well, it is well with my soul.

Doug got the message Jim was attempting to deliver to them through the choice of song, but, right now, in all honesty, it wasn't well with *his* soul.

Oh, yes, he was all right with Quinton Reed's death. That was well with his soul. Reed couldn't hurt anyone ever again. But Cynthia—the woman who had been his soul mate, who was supposed to walk through life by his side was gone forever. Forever. That wasn't at all well with his soul. His life and future without Cynthia was turned upside down. Every future goal or plan had now changed. He thought about Cynthia almost every minute of the day. He could envision her running through the woods in the dark – running for her life. Getting shot in the back like an animal. How can you find peace knowing that?

Doug knew he was supposed to be accepting of God's will, but it was so hard. He was trying, however. He needed help from family, friends, and God, but he just wasn't there yet. And he didn't know if he could be the strong rock for his kids when he himself was struggling and needing strengthened. Right now, all he knew was that in this life, God wasn't through with him yet.

CHAPTER 42

The Conrad family returned to their home by 9:30 p.m. and decided to spend the last hour sitting in the family room reminiscing about Cynthia, Quinton Reed, and their future goals as independent adults but also as a family. Snuggles curled up beside Taylor and put her head in her lap. Taylor caressed her ears and before long Snuggles had fallen asleep. She was such a sweet and loving dog. Everyone loved Snuggles.

In their conversation, neither of the children felt it necessary to continue counseling, but Doug wasn't sure about Taylor. Both kids were anchored in their faith, but Taylor had been kidnapped and was seconds away from being murdered by Reed. Even worse, his blood splattered all over her and part of his body slumped on top of her as he fell dead. That had to affect her. The scene was horrific for him as he could only stand there and watch, but his 19 year old daughter was a very emotional and demonstrative female. After all, it was fear for her father's safety that brought her home that night, when she was ordered by him to stay at the police station where she could be protected. Could she work through this alone? He planned to keep in touch with her daily and observe her silently.

Once again he knew his children would be walking out the door tomorrow morning to return to their life away from home. The house would once again be quiet, too quiet. For a long time, now, it had been missing laughter, and light-hearted, sweet-spirited pranks that were common in the Conrad home, and, most of all, the unashamed expressions of love and hugs and kisses. Doug didn't want this evening to end. Having the kids home was awesome and comforting to him.

They went through at least fifteen photograph books, reliving various holidays spent as a family—Mother's Day, Father's Day, Fourth of July, Labor Day, birthday parties, high school graduations, backyard picnics, vacations, and more. It was a lifetime of fun and the sweetest of memories. Much of those memories brought robust laughter. It was such a happy diversion for all three of them. None of them wanted the evening to end, but tomorrow was a school day for both Taylor and Paul, and Paul had a two hour drive to Columbus. They had all agreed to rise early and eat a hearty breakfast at Friendly's before going their separate ways.

When Doug closed his bedroom door after kissing Paul and Taylor goodnight, he felt a burden lifted. Perhaps it was all the laughter tonight—despite their sadness, all three were able to laugh. Some of the incidents Paul and Taylor had recalled from their childhood were hilarious!

You would be so proud of our kids right now, Cynthia! They have your indomitable spirit.

CHAPTER 43

Donna Gifford sat in her office with a light on perusing through some research she had done regarding PAS—parental alienation syndrome.

She needed to take her mind off killing Quinton Reed, so she delved into the Chandler case. If Bill and Rita Chandler had a messy divorce, Andy, their only son, would surely have been put right in the middle of their bitterness, most likely. One study showed of 700 high conflict divorces followed over a twelve year period, that PAS was present in the vast majority of those cases. One parent turning their child against the other parent isn't a complicated concept at all, but it's not always easy to identify. Donna learned that there were four very specific criteria used to identify PAS:

Number 1 was the active blocking access or contact between the child and the absent or non-custodial parent. The custodial parent treats the absent parent as merely an annoying acquaintance that the child must see at times. As a result, that parent isn't treated as a key family member. Over time that pattern could have a seriously erosive effect on the child's relationship with that absent parent. In this case, Bill. The child starts to interpret the situation of the parent visitation as an errand or chore or an *inconvenience.* So the child views the one parent superior—that would be Rita—to the absent parent, Bill.

Having read through more of Ivy's journals, she found numerous incidents where Rita had barred Bill from speaking to Andy on the phone when he called the house to talk to his son. When Bill would drive to the house for his mid-week visitation, no one would be found at home. Rita would later claim they had forgotten it was Wednesday visitation and, besides, *Andy wanted to go over to his friend's house to play* or Rita needed to take him shopping for some school shoes, which he needed badly. Visitation had slipped both of their minds. *Yeah, right, Rita.* No one in his right mind would buy into that tale. Ivy wrote of many incidents like that and, of course, not once did Rita allow Bill to have another day with Andy for makeup.

The second criteria was about *unfounded abuse allegations.* Usually the custodial parent would accuse the absent parent of sexual abuse. Rarely would physical abuse be used if no bruises or injuries were ever witnessed by third parties. Sometimes emotional abuse is leveled but that could be just differing parental judgment calls and called *abusive* by the custodial parent. For instance, if the absent parent had a *"significant other"* before the custodial parent thought he should, that parent would suggest it is abusive to the child. Or if a child is enrolled in an activity by one parent and the other parent disapproves of that activity—the difference of parental opinion—that could be considered *abusive* in nature. It may even seem like a trivial disagreement where one parent displays inappropriate subjective judgmental terms, but the emotional atmosphere that it creates carries a clearly alienating effect on the child. Sometimes the custodial parent will sign the child up for an activity simply because he knows the other parent would be adamantly opposed to it, and it's a way of getting under the absent parent's skin and demonstrating control.

From the journals, Rita clearly did that. Andy was allowed to ride and even drive a four wheeler at a young age in the woods. While she assured Bill he wore a helmet at all times, Bill worried Andy would fall off and get injured. Andy bragged about how fast they went in the woods. Out of the mouth of babes . . .

According to Ivy's journal, they learned through friends that Rita had told many different people about town that *Bill had physically abused her and that he had a very mean spirit. Thus, the cause of the divorce.* That couldn't have been further from the truth. Her infidelity was really the cause. Ivy called Bill her *gentle giant.*

Every employee who worked for Bill that she and Barnabus had interviewed had mentioned what a gentle, kind man Bill was, so it appeared Rita had set out to deliberately defame Bill's character throughout the community and make herself a *victim.* If she told outsiders these embellished stories, then she surely told those stories within earshot of Andy. And who wouldn't believe his own mother? Rita probably told her stories with such believability that it brought her sympathy. Ivy indicated Rita had told such stories to people in Rita's church, at her hair salon for her cosmetologist and all of the patrons to hear, and to professional people such as her dentist and ophthalmologist. If Andy had heard these stories over and over again, what would he be feeling toward his dad? Anger?

The third criteria necessary for PAS was the deterioration in the relationship after it had been a positive one. A decision in the relationship doesn't just *happen on its own.* Something caused it to change. Children don't naturally lose interest in their parent simply because that parent was the non-residential parent. The relationship was *attacked.*

From Ivy's journal, Andy and Bill had a loving relationship. Ivy's presence never changed that. In fact, Andy had welcomed her into the home with open arms and the three of them got along famously. So what happened between the age of three and fifteen to change that, Donna wondered.

Oftentimes the residential parent acts like the relationship has always been strained and this is just a continuation of what has already existed between the child and the parent.

According to the journal, Rita had gone to court in an effort to reduce—more likely squelch—Bill's visitation times. She wasn't successful in court, even though she had pulled Andy out of school to testify that he no longer desired visitation with his father. The judge disallowed Andy's testimony, thus thwarting Rita's devious plan. Bill and Ivy didn't even know Andy had been hidden away in a back room of the courthouse by Rita's lawyer until the request was made to bring Andy in to share his wishes. Bill and Ivy were deeply hurt and devastated by Rita's attempt. Did Andy really want this or was he simply trying to please his mother? Either way, it was emotionally painful for Bill. Ivy ached for both Bill and Andy. They could only imagine the fear and discomfort this was for Andy.

The final criteria pertained to the child wanting to please the residential parent, even if it was more out of fear than of his own volition. The child fears if he doesn't follow his residential parent's directives, he will be alienated from that parent too. The child is put through loyalty tests by the residential parent and it is solely fear-based. The child lives in a state of chronic upset and threat as he is forced to choose which parent of the two he will devote his loyalty. Since the child is afraid of *abandonment*, he realizes there will be serious reprisals if he chooses the *absent* parent. So then the child changes his behavior toward the absent parent so as not to displease the alienating parent. There are such sudden changes in the child for no apparent reason during visitation, it is observable to the visiting parent. An example might be that the child will protest an appointed visit to the absent parent when he had not previously complained about it before. The alienating parent acts bewildered by the child's desire not to visit the absent parent when, in fact, it had been deliberately staged for that end result.

Sometimes a child is given significant choice in the visitation and to prove his loyalty will choose to not have the visitation at all. The child then begins to learn to manipulate, pitting the parents against each other. They learn to read the emotional barometer of the situation, telling partial truths to the absent parent or even blatant lies. It's a survival strategy that the child is forced to learn in order to keep peace at home. It then becomes so much easier for the child to internalize the alienating parent's perception of the other parent. In a very short time, the child begins to vilify the absent parent. In court it is often hard for a domestic court judge to know if this is the child's true feelings and perceptions of the other parent OR if the child has been brainwashed and makes such negative comments out of fear of alienation.

Well, as Donna read the description of PAS, it was clear Rita understood the concepts exceedingly well and had refined the techniques of alienating Andy from his father . . . and stepmother. From the time he was a young child, Andy had been bamboozled, if Ivy's journals were to be believed.

CHAPTER 44

Several days had passed since Quinton Reed had been killed in Doug Conrad's front yard. Doug had spent time with Taylor and Paul trying to calm down and assess all of the emotional damage Reed had wreaked on him and his family so that they could move on with their lives.

While Doug had witnessed terrible crimes because of his career, it was different when it touched your life so personally. Doug worried that Paul and Taylor—especially Taylor—would have emotional issues as they desperately attempted to put this tragic ordeal behind them. As Jim Pascoe said to him after he confided of his deep concern for his children's mental well-being, *"Worrying doesn't take away tomorrow's troubles, Doug. It takes away today's peace. Turn it over to God."*

Doug was trying to do that. It wasn't easy, no matter how much support you were given by friends and family. He was thankful he had so many good friends, both old and new. Fearing that Doug was going to struggle with his situation alone and hold everything inside as many men tend to do, Jim recently reminded him, *"Old friends are gold while the new ones are the diamonds. If you get a diamond, don't forget the gold because to hold the diamond, you always need the gold base."* Doug could never forget any of his friends. He relished them.

Jim Pascoe and Mitch Neubauer were his two oldest and most dependable friends, and now Barnabus Johnson and Donna Gifford had come into his life and had already shared one of the most personal and emotional moments of his life, even to the point of risking their lives for him.

Doug's heart had been broken over the loss of Cynthia. How can your heart not break when you lose a loved one? Broken hearts are what give people strength, understanding, and even compassion. They give you purpose to your life. The heart that has never been broken is pristine and sterile and will never know the joy of being imperfect. These friends had touched his heart in an unspeakable way.

So now it was time to go to work and help another family who had also suffered a family loss and had not yet seen their murders vindicated.

Doug called a morning meeting to discuss the Chandler case. Mitch, Barnabus, and Donna Gifford were sitting around the table as Doug stepped into the conference room with a bag of freshly baked pastries from Panera Bread and Jean brought in a coffee pot of freshly brewed Folgers for everyone.

CHAPTER 45

D oug asked each one of his detectives to share information they had been working on regarding the Chandler case. Donna Gifford had briefly explained parental alienation syndrome and how this could very well play into the angle that Andy might be the *prime* suspect in the Chandler case. Right from the very beginning, Donna believed that the son was somehow involved in the murders. Doug, being the father of a son, was hoping she was wrong, but, admittedly, knew that Andy could have a motive, despite being estranged from his father and stepmother for ten years.

Barnabus—well, Zap, as he preferred to be called—discussed serial killers, a possibility suggested by Dr. Brandon White. In April 2011, a serial killer named Edward Edwards from Akron was executed after pleading guilty to five slayings in Ohio and Wisconsin. He murdered his foster son and a young couple who were sweethearts. He shot them at point-blank range with a 20 gauge shotgun. He later killed another couple in Wisconsin that he didn't even know. He bragged about his life of crime. How many more people he killed would never be known, so the theory of a serial killer was still feasible. Edwards was in prison at the time of these murders, but certainly there are people who kill couples they don't even know, shooting them at close range, for no reason whatsoever except that they can. Zap reminded them that Jeffrey Dahmer grew up in the Summit County/Akron area so Akron was no stranger to serial killers.

"If we search for a serial killer in the Chandler case, it will be like trying to find a needle in a haystack. A guy who might just be passing through the state, has no motive for killing the Chandlers, appears normal, and never brags of his kill." Do we really want to invest our time looking at this angle was the question Zap posed.

Mitch had been following the daily habits and routines of some of the feasible suspects in this case. He learned which proprietors they did business with frequently, where they worked, and who they played with as well as places they visited frequently. It was a lot of footwork and phone calls. Clearly people who came into contact with them could provide an honest perspective to that person's capabilities and involvement in the case.

Mitch began discussing Andy's daily routine. Andy was living on the second floor of the Harding Apartments in Akron, not far from the Ellet district where he grew up. He works at Akron General Medical Center as a hospital business office clerk, working in medical data systems. It was an office job that paid about $23,000 a year. Andy had chosen not to attend college. He had always hated school and had never really applied himself since his elementary school days. He rarely got a grade above a C and more often than not, barely passed most of his classes. That alone reduced many of the quality jobs available to him. Andy had never shown an interest in physical labor either, so jobs such as construction or factory work were not up for his consideration. Andy loves toys. He owns a used Silverado truck and a 2011 Harley-Davidson Sportster SuperLow XL883L. He is a member of the YMCA. He visits the gym at least three evenings a week to swim and work out. He has rekindled a relationship with an old high school sweetheart and it is believed he might even be engaged to her. Each have their own place, but there are obvious sleepovers. His girlfriend or fiancee's name is Wendy Graves. She works as a retail clerk in housewares at Macy's department store at Summit Mall.

Mitch then moved on to Rita Marie Morgan Darrington, Bill Chandler's ex-wife. She married Chaz Darrington, a seemingly wealthy insurance agent for Nationwide. Rita goes weekly for a manicure, a pedicure, and a full body massage. She gets her hair fixed every Thursday morning at Classic Hair Salon. She shops and quite often buys herself an expensive piece of jewelry. She drives around in her BMW, looking very important. There is nothing the Darringtons *don't* have, so it seems. They live in a $450,000 home with a four car garage. The house has an underground swimming pool in their two acre backyard, which has a posh, well-groomed patio enclosed by a private white picket fence.

The happily married couple also owns a Toyota Land Cruiser SUV, two sports cars—Rita's blue BMW and Chaz's silver Jaguar. They also own a 4x4 truck along with two four-wheelers and two Jet Skis. They keep a ski boat docked at Sandy Beach Marina. They have a Doberman pinscher. So the Darringtons don't deny themselves anything. They live a very ostentatious lifestyle. They boast a lot about their material wealth. The insurance business is a lucrative career, but it is hard to fathom that they could afford all of those top quality possessions on only one person's income. Of course for years the Darringtons who were custodial parents of Andy and Chaz's three kids received child support from both ex-spouses. Both were sizable, but, now that all the kids are grown and out of the nest, they are no longer receiving the tax free child support payments. And, yet, the Darringtons continue to live the lavish life.

If the Darringtons were in debt or living far above their means, they still wouldn't be prime suspects in the crime as it appeared the Chandler home had not been burglarized and nothing of great value appeared to be missing. Now if the Darringtons wanted to avenge a wrong done to them by the Chandlers, revenge could be the motive, but nothing in the police report pointed to that. Nevertheless, the team decided not to rule out Rita or Chaz just yet.

From Ivy's journal readings, Rita spewed vitriolic words to Bill almost everytime they shared a phone conversation about Andy. There was a lot of underlying anger, but where it came from was anyone's guess as Rita's infidelity resulted in the marriage break-up.

Rita would need to be scrutinized more carefully. Perhaps a link in this crime chain was being missed. Mitch agreed they should dig deeper into Rita's relationship to the Chandlers.

Chaz Darrington, before marrying Rita, would never have been up for the Father of the Year award according to Amy, his ex-wife. He seldom took an interest in their lives or school activities. He had affairs over the course of their marriage, so he had not really been there for her either. According to Amy, Chaz was digging them into a deep financial hole with all his reckless and foolish spending. He wore so many gold chains around his neck, he looked like Mr. T. For quite some time she actually thought Chaz was raking in the money as they were able to maintain an affluent lifestyle. Chaz took care of paying all of the bills, so she didn't learn until after they had separated just how deep in debt they actually were from all of their spending.

CHAPTER 46

Donna Gifford was browsing through the housewares department at Macy's, looking as though she was confused or undecided. Exactly as hoped for, Wendy Graves, the clerk walking around straightening displays spotted her and walked over to her.

"*Is there something I could help you with?*" she asked sincerely.

"*I hope you can. I want to buy a wedding gift for a niece who lives out of the States, and I'm not sure what to get her.*"

"*Where does she live out of the States?*"

"*Well, she's engaged to a guy in the military and right now they're in Germany living together off base, but I'm not sure for how long. He may soon be deployed to Afghanistan, so they want to get married before he has to leave.*"

"*Well, did you have something in mind?*"

"*Not really. She's young. Probably close to your age, so I imagine she needs about everything.*"

"*Well, you're probably right about that. I'm 25 years old and engaged to be married in several months myself, and I need almost everything.*"

"*Is she registered in any stores that you know of?*"

"*No, she's not registered with anyone. I think probably anything I get her would be needed and greatly appreciated. By their setting up house early, however, I don't know what she might already have.*"

"I live with my fiancé too. Well, not all of the time. I actually have my own apartment I share with two girlfriends, but I stay over with him when my girlfriends bug me and I need to get away from them."

"So who's your lucky guy?"

"Andy Chandler, an old high school friend," she proudly responded. Donna Gifford smiled at her phrase *'old high school friend."*

"Chandler. That name sounds familiar."

"Andy's dad was murdered several months ago. You may have read about it in the paper."

"How horrible! Especially since you're getting married soon. That must be awful for your fiancé. Andy is his name?"

"Yes. Well, not really. Andy wasn't close to his father. I don't think he planned to invite him to the wedding anyway."

"What about Andy's mother? Is she still alive?"

"Oh, yes. His parents were divorced a long time ago. Andy was about 4 years old when his parents divorced."

"Did they ever catch who killed his father?" Donna asked with curiosity.

"No, they haven't."

"These white Pfaltzgraff dishes. Are they microwavable?"

"Yes. That might be a good choice, but shipping to Germany would be expensive."

"Yes, you're right. Let's keep looking."

"Well, does your fiancé have any ideas who killed his dad?"

"I don't think so. He hadn't seen his dad for nearly ten years, but he doesn't like to talk about it. Not even to me."

"Well, does Andy's mother have any ideas?"

"Not really. She said Bill—that was Andy's dad's name—was meaner than a snake and probably had lots of enemies who wanted to kill him. She said he probably got what he deserved."

"Ouch! I guess their divorce wasn't too amicable."

"No, it wasn't."

"So was Bill abusive to Andy while growing up?"

"If he was Andy never talked about it. Andy just mentioned that his dad mistreated his mom and that Bill's second wife was a living nightmare."

"So Andy—during his visitation—I suppose dreaded having to stay at his dad's house?"

"Well, I never heard him share specific bad experiences he had while visiting them, so I don't know what issues he had with them. I guess we just never talked about those years.

"What about this skillet set?" asked Wendy as they walked around the displays talking and looking at the various kitchen items.

Donna looked at the total cost for the complete set.

"Oh, my, I think I'm going into sticker shock. This is a little pricier than my budget can afford.

"As an older person, could I make a suggestion to you?" Donna asked.

"Sure. What?"

"Before you marry Andy, inquire a lot more about his family background. It sounds like he could have some deep-seated issues from his youth with his parents. Sometimes anger management becomes a latent problem as time goes on. Having a father murdered, I would think, would surely have an affect on him in some way, whether he's aware of it now or later.

"Had you ever met Andy's dad and stepmother?"

"No, but after they were murdered I—"

"What? The stepmother was murdered too?"

"Oh, yes. I guess I didn't mention that. Well, anyway, I went with Andy to the funeral home the evening of the viewing so I saw them for the first time—of course, they were dead."

"So how did Andy do with seeing them both dead?"

"Actually, he seemed unmoved. He didn't want to linger at the funeral home. He paid his respects, but I think he felt uncomfortable around the family members since Andy chose NOT to see Bill and Ivy since he was 15 years old."

"Well, you are a brave girl for walking into a family with such serious issues. I would learn as much as I could about Andy and his mother before joining the family."

"Well, I think I know them pretty well. I try not to pry into the crime as I'm sure it is such a sensitive topic to Andy."

"I see your point. Just remember when you marry Andy, you are married into the family. Sounds like there is some emotional baggage that could surface that could complicate your relationship with Andy."

"What do you mean?" Wendy asked.

"I guess I mean Andy may have some deep regrets that he was never able to have a positive relationship with his dad and, now, he never will. If what I hear you saying, his dad was okay with him, but he harbored ill-will against his dad based on how Bill treated his mother. And, if they were divorced when Andy was only 4, would Andy really remember witnessing his dad's abuse toward his mom? He's basing it only on what his mom told him."

"Yeah, I guess you're right. Hmmmm! There are probably two sides to every story. I probably need to talk to Andy more about his childhood. You make a good point."

"Well, I'm guessing Andy is a heck of a nice guy or a sweet girl like you wouldn't have fallen for him."

"Yes, he is a nice guy," she smiled sweetly. *"We're getting married in November—Thanksgiving weekend."*

"Awesome! Well, good luck to you," Donna responded. *"You know, the more I'm looking at all of these great housewares, I get even more undecided. I probably should have called my sister for some suggestions for a much needed gift. She would surely know what they could use. I'm so sorry to take up so much of your time, but it was fun talking to you, Wendy."*

"Business is slow this evening, so this helps to pass the time. I'm always excited to talk about my fiancé as I guess most brides-to-be are. It was nice talking to you. I hope you come back with your list when I'm here so I can help you."

"I hope so too, Wendy. Are you on commission?"

"No, but I like to help people."

"I know what you mean. So do I. Good luck to you, and if we don't meet again, have a lovely wedding. You will make a beautiful bride."

"Thanks!"

As Donna walked away, she felt she had obtained some interesting perspectives from Wendy. The girl was definitely naïve—typical for the age, perhaps—and quite loquacious. She would definitely be returning to housewares sometime.

CHAPTER 47

Barnabus arrived at the YMCA and changed into his workout clothes. The lockers were almost all taken, so he knew it would be challenging to get on certain machines he wanted. He entered the fitness area and began with the EFX835 Elliptical Fitness Crosstrainer for stretching. As he was moving with the machine, his eyes were moving around the room until he spotted Andy three machines over, working out on the RevMaster. A PaceMaster right next to him had just been freed up so Barnabus made his way over to it. He looked totally focused on his exercise regime. Barnabus had been so well trained in the U.S. Marines that he was devoted to a daily arduous and rigorous exercise program. He could do one hundred push ups and not even break a sweat. It was nothing for him to do fifty laps in the pool without needing a break. Very few of the jocks who go to gyms to work out could maintain the rigorous workout that was mundane for Barnabus, and he knew it.

Barnabus set his program on the steepest incline key he could to elevate the highest heart rate.

He could feel Andy's stare. Andy noticed the T-shirt Barnabus was wearing which said, *"The Few. The Proud. The Marines."*

"So you were a marine?" asked Andy.

Barnabus looked straight ahead, pretending not to notice that Andy was speaking to him.

"So you were a Marine?" asked Andy again but a bit louder the second time.

Barnabus purposefully looked a bit surprised at the interruption.

"Oh, are you talkin' to me?" he asked.

"Yes. Were you a marine?"

"Yes, sir, I was."

"How long?"

"Ten years."

"Yeah? Did you get to travel around?"

"Sure did." Barnabus not wanting to look like he was interested in engaging in a conversation with Andy made him dig for answers.

"Like where?" Andy asked.

"Well, Yemen, Iraq, and Iran for starters."

'What was your rank?"

"Military police."

"Wow!" Andy looked at him with admiration.

"You interested in the Marines?"

"Well, I was, but it didn't work out for me."

"Too bad. The marines offer recruits great training, awesome experiences, and good benefits. The chicks in the program are pretty admirable as well."

"What is your name?" Andy asked.

"Barnabus, but my nickname is Zap."

"Zap?"

"Got nicknamed that by my superior officer."

"How did you get that name?"

"If I told you, I'd have to kill ya!" Then Barnabus broke out in his raucous laugh.

"No, I'm just kidding, but it would take too long to share the story."

"So, what's your name?" Barnabus asked.

"Andy."

"So what do you do, Andy?"

"I'm a medical data systems clerk at Akron General Medical Center."

"Ah, so you sit at a desk all day. That's why you need to come and work out, eh? Pretty sedentary job?"

"Yes, you can say that again!"

"Pretty sedentary job, eh?" They both laughed at the repeat. Andy couldn't stop laughing at Zap's funny laugh.

Barnabus moved to the Precor Super Bench, set his weights and spent the next 5-7 minutes working his chest, shoulders, biceps, and triceps. He noticed Andy watching him. As he moved to the Ab-X machine, Andy came over and got on the Ab-X next to him. It was a focused abdominal workout, but Andy quit long before Barnabus did.

Feeling like Andy was trying to compete with him, Barnabus walked over to him:

"I work out once, sometimes, twice a day, Andy. It's something you have to build up to in order to have my kind of stamina. The military requires and actually instills a rigorous workout regime in every marine so that it almost becomes a way of life for us.

"Since I'm not married and don't have a family, I have lots of free time to work out. And, who knows, maybe I'll meet a good lookin' chick here who recognizes me for the charming, good looking homosapien that I am!" Barnabus broke out in his rip-roaring laugh that made Andy start laughing again.

"You come here to find you a healthy, voluptuous girl, Andy?" Barnabus inquired.

"No. Actually I'm engaged."

"Oh yeah? When you tying the knot?"

"In a few months."

"Want to join me for a protein shake or a fusion at the health bar?" Barnabus asked.

"Sure."

As they sipped on their health drinks, Barnabus asked,

"So did you grow up around here?"

"Yeah, I grew up in Ellet as a kid and then my parents divorced. My mom remarried and then eventually we moved to Fairlawn."

"You still live with your mom?"

"Oh, no. I moved out as soon as I graduated from high school and could make it on my own."

"So you live in an apartment?"

"Yeah. I live in the Harding Apartments in Springfield Township near the Ellet border. It's more convenient to get to my fiancee's apartment from there.

"Do you have a roommate you share expenses with?"

"No. I tried that for awhile, but I prefer to live alone, even if it helped financially to split the rent with someone."

"So did your dad remarry?" Back to the Chandlers again with Barnabus's redirection.

"Yeah, eventually."

"So do they live nearby to lend you a hand?"

"No. My dad and his wife are now deceased."

"Oh, I'm sorry. May I ask what happened?" Barnabus asked sincerely, even though he knew the answer.

"No one knows."

"What do you mean?"

"They were both found dead in the basement."

"So what was it? Carbon monoxide?"

"No. Actually, they were murdered."

It was clear to Barnabus that Andy was reluctant to provide details even though he probably knew most or all of them. Barnabus studied his countenance which appeared stoic for such a tragic incident.

"I'm sorry. Did this happen a long time ago?"

"Several months back."

"So did they catch who did it?"

"Not that I know of," responded Andy.

"I bet you can't rest in peace until the police catch who did it."

"Actually, I can. I wasn't close to my dad and I didn't like Ivy. That was his wife."

"And your stepmother." Barnabus added to see his reaction.

"I never looked at her that way. She was a nonentity to me."

"Really? Why was that?"

"She just was." Andy was looking exceedingly uncomfortable as Barnabus tried to press on for more information. He didn't want to push Andy too far. Hopefully, there would be more opportunities to pry more information out of him.

"Well, I'm really sorry for your loss. I hope you find closure somewhere down the road."

"Yeah, thanks."

They slurped their cranberry fusions in silence for awhile. Barnabus could see Andy was now deep in thought and looked troubled. Very troubled.

Well, guess I'd better get on home. Perhaps we'll see each other back here another time."

"Sure thing, Zap! But I gotta hear about how you got named Zap next time."

"Okay."

Barnabus showered and changed back into his black cargo pants and a black t-shirt. He looked at the clock on the dash of his Miata. It was 9:10 p.m. He decided to tail Andy to see where his next destination was. He would try to stay far behind.

Andy pulled out of the YMCA. He appeared to be engrossed in deep thought. He was driving a rusty Silverado truck. Andy obeyed all of the traffic signs and signals and maintained a lawful speed, especially for a young guy. Perhaps much of that was due to the age of the car rather than that of the driver. Nevertheless, Barnabus was impressed with Andy.

Andy took a right turn down Caston Road and then a left on South Main Street. There wasn't much traffic on the road at that time of evening. An adult baseball team was enjoying its victory ice cream social at the corner ice cream stand. Barnabus tried to lag far behind watching Andy turn right onto Center Road. He crossed over Manchester Road, staying on Center Road. As he got more familiar with the area, Barnabus realized that Andy was heading for Bill and Ivy Chandler's home.

Had he and Andy not had the conversation about Bill Chandler at the snack bar, would Andy have chosen to drive by his father's old house? Probably not. He really lagged behind and cut his headlights off.

Andy drove to the Chandler house and parked at the bottom of the driveway. Because it was so dark, Barnabus wasn't sure, but he thought Andy was draped over his steering wheel and perhaps weeping.

But were they tears of sadness or guilt? That's what Conrad Confidential had to figure out. Barnabus drove passed the Chandler home and headed for his own condo.

CHAPTER 48

Donna Gifford was sitting in a stylist chair getting her hair cut, permed, and set. She had deliberately arranged her appointment to coincide with Rita Darrington's hair appointment. In fact, Donna had been so fastidious in her plan, she knew she needed Carla to do her hair so she would be at the chair beside Kim's station. Every Thursday morning Rita came to get her hair cut or styled by Kim and her nails manicured.

It would be a natural, unsuspecting setting, and she was sure she could engage Rita in a conversation about Bill and Ivy Chandler.

Donna and Rita coincidentally arrived at Classic Hair Salon at the same time. As they got to the door simultaneously, it was clear from Rita's body language that she expected to enter the salon first—perhaps due to a *royalty* or *"I'm more important than you"* attitude. Donna comfortably conceded to Rita with a smile and a friendly hello.

Not really paying attention to the other, both ladies were called to the stylist chair by their cosmetologists. Capes were being wrapped around them and the usual small talk began.

Donna explained what she wanted done to her hair. Carla, her stylist, listened attentively and set her station up with scissors and curlers and perm solution. Not wanting to waste any time, Donna proceeded to tell Carla a preconceived story about her dear friend who had a small child and was in the process of a divorce. She told this story using enough volume so that Rita and her stylist, Kim, could hear. She was hoping they were eavesdropping, and sure enough, they were. Kim immediately spoke up.

"Well, Rita, here, is the queen of the hill when it comes to dealing with divorce. Aren't you, Rita? Like your friend, Rita went through a lot."

"I sure am," replied Rita. *"I could write a book on divorce."*

"What makes it so hard on my friend is that she has a young child, and she really needs to find a job pretty quickly," responded Donna.

"Wrongo!" spoke Rita spontaneously. *"That's actually the last thing she needs to do. Trust me. If she has a good lawyer, he will tell her not to work. She will get more alimony and support from her husband. Make the louse pay!"* And with that Rita laughed loudly.

"Yes, but I think the courts will impute a certain amount from her regardless."

"Yes, they do now, but they didn't used to. Not when I was going through the court system, so she needs to find a not-so-good doctor and start faking some medical problems to support the fact that she is unable to work. Then she can really screw her husband over."

"You think THAT will really work?"

"I know it will, girl!"

Donna could see that Rita was on a roll and enjoying every minute of this conversation, so she continued to encourage her to talk more.

"So is her child a boy or girl?"

"He's a boy."

"How old?"

"I think he's either in kindergarten or starting first grade."

"Well, it's good she's getting the divorce now while the son is so young."

"Really? I'd think that was worse."

"No, not at all. Now your girlfriend can start programming her son."

"Programming?"

"Well, the husband is a creep or she wouldn't be divorcing him, right?"

"I'm not really sure what their problems were. She's kind of a private person."

"Well, her problems will get worse if she lets her husband get too much control of the kid. She doesn't want the kid to want to go live with the dad somewhere down the line, so she needs to start programming this kid so that that never happens."

"So how should she go about that?" asked Donna sincerely.

"Well, since the boy's so young and may not know when to keep quiet, she needs to start by spending lots of time with him, doing things he likes to do."

"I think she does that."

"Oh, yes, but she should keep telling him how important he is to her—the most important thing in her life and how she couldn't live without him. Keep instilling that thought. Then when the father comes for his mid-week visitation, let him know how much she missed him when he was gone."

Then Rita started laughing as she was reminiscing.

"My new husband and some of his children and I would go do something 'kid fun' and go on and on about it when my son came home from his midweek visitation with his dad. Eventually, the son won't look forward to going with his dad and will want to go off with the mom and stepdad."

"But why would you want to do that? Isn't it healthy for a kid to feel loved by both parents?" asked Donna.

"Well, my husband was so abusive that I didn't want my son to be around him. Plus he now has a new and better dad. That's all he needed."

"Oh, well, that's kind of different. My friend's husband wasn't abusive. Did your ex-husband hurt your son?"

"No, but he was physically, mentally, verbally, and emotionally abusive to me."

"I'm so sorry. Did you have police reports and get a restraining order on him for those abuses?"

"No, but I should have."

"Did your son witness those abuses? I know that can be so upsetting to a child."

"No, but I made sure my son knew what his father did to me and what he was capable of doing."

"So your son must have been scared to spend weekends with his dad."

"Eventually he didn't want to go see him anymore. He dreaded the visits. He wanted to stay at home with us. We had become one big happy family, so my ex—husband was simply in the way.

"My ex-husband was quite wealthy, but so is my new husband, so we had the monetary power to challenge my ex in court for things and buy things for our son that Bill—that was my ex-husband—refused to get him or didn't approve of."

"Hmmm. So all of that worked?"

"Well, Bill loved our son and didn't give up easily. But Chaz and I—Chaz is my new husband—did so many devious things to wear Bill down that Bill finally got discouraged and as our son got older he started making excuses for not spending weekends with his dad and the new stepmother."

"Bill remarried?"

"Well, eventually. Bill married a school teacher. My son hated school so on that basis alone he didn't like Ivy Connivy from the get-go."

"Her name was Ivy Connivy?" Donna asked.

"No," Rita laughed. *"That's what we called her in our home."*

"Did your son know what conniving meant?"

"We taught him the word, and let's just say it stuck with him." Rita cackled again. She was enjoying reliving these moments and seemed totally unabashed about doing such things and letting others know she had done them. Donna wondered what the other people in the salon thought as they listened to Rita talk. The stylists had obviously heard these stories before and listened with *sympathy*

"Ivy was always trying to plan some fun vacation for our son—I'm sure in an effort to win his heart over—but we thwarted her every effort."

"How did you do that?"

"Bill was required to ask me for specific vacation weeks. Like when it was his turn to have Andy for spring break, he was required by law to tell me where he was taking Andy. Andy's my son.

"So when he would supply the details, we would pull Andy out of school the week before their vacation and take him there ourselves. By the time Bill got him the following week, Andy didn't want to go there again and was bored. There wasn't a thing Bill or Ivy could do about it."

"When our son played soccer, I would give Bill a fake soccer schedule that I had typed up. I sent him to the wrong soccer fields, so he wouldn't know where Andy was playing and would miss the game. Bill was pretty sharp, though, and he would quickly find out where Andy was actually playing and show up ten minutes late.

"So, in the end, I got even with my evil ex."

"So does your son have a relationship with his dad now?"

"Well, no, but that's for two reasons. As soon as Andy became a teenager and had more say in his life, especially after he got his driver's license at sixteen, he stopped going over to his father's for weekend visitations. He wanted to be with his friends. Bill never fought it because he would have had to go to court and fight that, and he knew he probably wouldn't win.

"Secondly, my husband and his wife are both dead."

"Both of them?" Donna asked in shock.

"Yep, both of them!" Rita said it as though she was pleased.

"What happened?" asked Donna.

"They were murdered, which doesn't necessarily surprise me."

"Was it a murder-suicide?" asked Donna.

"Oh, no. As I said, my husband was abusive and always had something hateful to say. He probably crossed the wrong person. OR, Ivy probably riled the wrong student. I'm sure they both made lots of enemies. Whatever happened, they got what they had coming to them." Rita said it without any remorse or sympathy toward them. It came across to Donna as terribly cold-hearted.

"So they didn't catch who did it?"

"No, they didn't. It didn't happen that long ago, but I suspect Andy should be coming in for a pretty hefty inheritance once things settle down. Bill owned his own business, which was quite lucrative, and Ivy didn't have any children. Andy was Bill's only son so I'm sure Bill would have

made Andy his beneficiary. I always told Andy, 'Your dad is as cheap as they come, but someday you will get what's coming to you as will he.'"

"Donna, I'm going to need you under the hairdryer for about thirty minutes," said Carla.

"No problem." Donna had heard plenty to get an impression of Rita. She would be back next week and could probably glean even more. Rita was quite a talker and thoroughly enjoyed sharing her life . . . as she saw it.

"Nice talking to you. I will share this information with my friend."

"You do that. It will make life easier for her, for sure. And she will be uno numero in her son's eyes forever!" retorted Rita.

Forty minutes later Donna drove away from Classic Hair Salon, satisfied with the outcome of her hair and the information gleaned from Rita Darrington. Donna pondered many things Rita told her as she unabashedly shared the devious acts she pulled on her ex-husband. It was obvious she loved having a captive audience. It was also clear the regular clients in the salon had heard Rita's story before and even seemed sympathetic with her. Of course, they accepted all of Rita's statements as factual. If they knew that Bill Chandler had been nothing but a loving husband and father, they most likely wouldn't have been supportive.

Donna also concluded that Rita actually seemed proud of distancing her son from his father. It was something hard for Donna to fathom. She wondered if perhaps this woman with the devious mind hadn't been the one to end Bill's life. After all, she made the comment 'T*hey got what they had coming to them.'* And when Andy was young—years before the Chandlers were murdered, she told Andy he *would someday get what's coming to him just as his father would. Was she being prophetic or simply second guessing the future?* Rita was quite aware that Andy was likely to be the beneficiary of some of Bill's wealth one day. However, that might only happen if his wife wasn't around to collect. And if Ivy wasn't around, Andy might get it all. So could the two of them possibly be in collusion?

CHAPTER 49

It was Saturday and Andy had the day off work. Wendy had to work at Macy's until 3:00 p.m., so Andy spent the morning washing his car, taking some shirts to the cleaners, and then working out at the Y.M.C.A. He wanted to drop at least ten pounds before the wedding.

Andy and Wendy had been looking forward to this date all week. They were driving up to Beachwood to have dinner at Cheesecake Factory. Afterward they planned on walking around Legacy Village to enjoy a leisurely stroll and the outdoor concert. Actually neither of them had much money to shop, so they mostly just browsed the shops. Someday, however, they would be financially set and would be able to buy anything they wanted, but for now they were saving almost every penny for wedding expenses.

Wendy wanted to eat outside. She looked so fresh and clean and feminine in her sundress. Andy pulled the chair out for her and kissed her on the cheek before seating himself. He felt so relaxed and without a care in the world. He looked across the table at Wendy's sweet smile and knew she shared the same dreams of their happy future as he did.

She reached across the table and held both of his hands after the waiter brought their Diet Cokes and had taken their dinner orders.

"When we mosey around this evening, I want to stop at Crate and Barrel and look for some unique kitchen utensils and things that we might want to register for."

"Sure," Andy replied.

"But right now, Andy, I've been thinking about some things that quite frankly have baffled me a little, and I need a little clarification."

"What about?" Andy asked.

"Your family."

"What about my family?" he asked inquisitively.

"Well, your family becomes my family after we're married, and there are so many things we haven't discussed that I'm curious about."

"Such as?"

"Well, you've never told me much about your dad."

"My real dad or stepdad?"

"No, your real dad."

"He's dead, so there's nothing to tell."

"Well, he didn't die until you were twenty-five years old, so you grew up with him as your father for most of your years. What was he like?"

"I don't like talking about my dad, Wendy. You know that," Andy replied, looking quite uncomfortable.

"I realize that, sweetie, but I believe his life had an influence on you, and I would simply like to know in what way, so I can know you better."

"What do you want to know about me?" he asked rather caustically.

Wendy sensed Andy's uneasiness and witnessed his agitation starting to build. His reticence was making her even more curious. The customer at the store the other day was correct when she told Wendy she should delve into her fiance's life regarding his family more.

"Well, what was your dad like?" asked Wendy with genuine curiosity.

"You are carrying some of his genes around, so I want to know what I'm getting." She laughed a little, hoping to lighten the now tense atmosphere a little.

"My dad owned his own business and worked and traveled a lot, so he was gone a day or two out of the week. He was usually home for the weekend, however."

It appeared to Wendy that Andy was done with the conversation. He was hoping that information would suffice and they could move on with something else. His avoidance of the topic was a curious point indeed.

"So did your dad take an interest in your life and support your activities?"

"By the time I got in kindergarten, my parents were divorced. Mom and I moved out of the house and into an apartment. My dad continued to live in the BIG house all by himself."

"Why was that?"

"As I found out later, Dad owned the house before he met Mom and the house was in his name only, so he opted to keep it and we had to move into a crumby apartment. Mom outsmarted him, however. She took almost everything Dad had in the house, so he mostly had just a roof over his head." Andy had a smile on his face as he said that.

"So how long did you have to live in that apartment?"

"Not too long really. My Mom started dating our former neighbor, and so we moved into a nicer apartment and he moved in with us. Of course, you know I'm talking about Chaz, my stepfather."

"So when did they finally marry?"

"It was about eight months later."

"That quickly?"

"It really wasn't that quickly. He was our neighbor. My mom had known him and his family for years. They had been our neighbors."

"I mean to fall in love that quickly after a divorce and actually marry."

Andy started looking uncomfortable with the underlying suggestion.

"My mom, remember, had been abused by my father for so long. Chaz was a breath of fresh air for her. He understood what my mother was going through."

"So she would talk to him about your dad?"

"I guess. I don't know, Wendy. I was only 3 or 4 years old!"

"So did your mom turn to her folks or siblings for help when your dad was abusing her?"

"Well, they knew about the abuse, but they didn't really step in to help. My mom was afraid of my dad. He had a violent temper. He threatened her more than physically hurt her, although he physically hurt her too."

"Did your mother ever call the police on him?"

"Not that I know of."

"Well, why not?" asked Wendy with such protectiveness.

"Did you ever see your dad hit your mom?" she asked.

"No."

"Did you ever hear him emotionally or verbally abuse her?"

"No. I think he did it when I was at pre-school or asleep in my room, but after we moved to the apartment, my mom told me all about what my dad did to her so I would understand why we had to move away. Then when Chaz moved in with us, Mom was a lot happier and felt safer," Andy responded defensively.

"So after you got in school, did your dad honor his visitations with you and show up for all of your school activities and sports events?"

"Well, we – Chaz and Mom and me—moved to a much nicer home in Ellet, which was across town from Dad. She got as far away as she could from Dad and then made him, through the courts, do all of the driving for visitation. Dad would come over and watch me play football, soccer, or track. He also came to all of the open houses and parent/teacher conferences at school, supposedly. He would tell me he went to those, but my Mom said he was a no show for most of them."

"But you know for sure he was at the sports events, right?"

"Oh, yes. He was there. But I would have preferred he not come."

"Why was that?"

"I was always afraid he and my Mom would get into an argument over a weekend visitation or something right there on the sidelines or in the bleachers."

"Had there been a problem to indicate that might happen?"

"No, but my Mom was always afraid. Chaz always tried to come along to the games to protect Mom and keep Dad away from us."

"From us? Meaning you too? Didn't your dad have a right as your father to talk to you?"

"What is your point, Wendy?" Andy asked angrily.

"I don't know, Andy. It just seems like if your dad took the time out of his busy schedule to come watch you play, he had a right to at least

speak to you before or after the game without being ignored or barred from speaking to you."

"Let's just drop it, okay?" Andy insisted.

"Okay. So when you spent weekends with your dad, what kinds of things did you do?"

"We did the typical things. We went to parks and raced my motorized cars and trucks or played basketball or went on a hike. Then later when Ivy came along, we spent more time at the house. Ivy would fix a nice meal and we would play games around the kitchen table. Maybe we would go see a movie or go for a walk around the neighborhood or fly a kite. Just lots of things."

"So it sounds like Ivy was a nice lady and stepmother to you?"

Andy rolled his eyes.

"My Mom couldn't stand her. Dad started giving my mom a harder time with visitation demands and wanting more vacation time, and Mom knew Ivy was behind it all."

"How did she know that?"

"I don't know, but she knew. Mom tried to spare me from all the ugly stuff. She fought them in court tooth and nail. Mom always won in court, so she had to be right."

"So, then, did you get to go on any vacations with your dad?"

"Oh, sure. We went to California once, Florida two times, Utah, Nevada, and Arizona on a trip to the West, and we even went on a cruise to Alaska, taking a train all the way up to Anchorage and Fairbanks."

"Wow! I would have loved that. I bet you had a ball!"

"Not really. My Mom had told me so many things my dad had done to her, I hated him by then. I didn't want to spend a second with him or Ivy Connivy. I actually despised them both."

"Ivy Connivy?" Wendy asked.

"That's what Mom and Chaz called her in our house. I started calling her that, too. Behind her back, of course." Andy kind of laughed under his breath as he thought about that.

"It's kind of denigrating to call your stepmother that, isn't it?"

"Well, I didn't call her that to her face. What she didn't know wouldn't hurt her."

"So, she was mean to you?"

Andy was taken back by that question. He hadn't given it any thought whatsoever.

"Hmmm. Well, Dad wasn't a disciplinarian, but Ivy was, so she was always making the rules. She was a school teacher, so she ran a tight ship in the house. That, of course, didn't sit well with my mother when she found out about that."

"What do you mean? How did she find out?"

"Well, when I would get back from visitation, she would ask me about the weekend. She would listen to me speak of what we did and then ask a lot of questions. When she found out that Ivy made me make my bed or clean up my room or give me chores to do over the short weekend, she was livid. Ivy didn't have a right to tell me what to do whatsoever."

"Well, she was your stepmother, wasn't she?"

"Yes. Step—mother. Not real mother," Andy replied defiantly.

"So, did Chaz tell you what to do when he moved in with you guys?"

"Yes, but that was different. He was now my new dad. He was living with us all the time and was the head of the house. He was supporting us."

"He's still a step—father, isn't he?" Wendy asked, pointing that out.

"He and my Mom were building a beautiful home—their dream home—for us—Chaz's kids—and then Mom got pregnant with Chaz, so a new baby was coming also. He was supporting all of us."

"So, wasn't your dad paying child support?"

"Supposedly, but my Mom had to go after him numerous times to provide support. She even had to take him to court because he was so behind in paying child support. He could easily have afforded to pay. He just didn't. He was mad because my Mom fell in love with Chaz and was finally happy."

"And you know that how?"

"Because my Mom told me!" Andy said to her with a frustrated and raised voice.

"Now can we please change the subject?" Andy asked.

"Sure." Wendy knew it was time to drop the touchy subject, but she had truly gleaned some interesting facts about what had happened that she didn't know before. She couldn't help but feel that there was so much more to learn here. The family dynamics were volatile, and Andy held such animosity toward his real father. And yet, Mr. Chandler actually sounded like a nice, caring father. Some of the facts didn't sound quite right, however. If Andy's dad cared enough about Andy to attend his activities and had a successful business, why would he avoid his child support at times? Perhaps there was more to this story than what she was being told. She knew that in the days ahead, she needed to learn more . . . and before she walked down the aisle to marry Andy.

CHAPTER 50

Mitch Neubauer stepped inside Ellet High School at 3:00 p.m. and signed in. He had made previous arrangements to meet with two of Andy's former teachers, his football coach, and the principal. He wanted to meet with each one separately. All three faculty members knew he was coming today after school and had arranged their schedules so they could meet in their classrooms as requested by Mr. Neubauer.

Mr. Maxwell, the high school principal walked up to Mr. Neubauer as he was signing into the building and pinning on his visitor's badge.

"Mr. Neubauer. I'm Christopher Maxwell, principal of Ellet High School. It's an honor to meet you. I followed the Doug Conrad case on TV and in the newspaper as most *Akronites did, and I want you to know how impressed I was with what you and your wife did to protect the Conrad kids. You are quite a hero.*

"I'll take you to the gym to meet with Andy's former football coach, Mr. Greg Kaiser. Mr. Kaiser has a meeting for all high school football coaches at four o'clock, so he needs to meet with you first so that he can leave for that meeting at Firestone High School."

"That would be fine," responded Mitch. *"Lead the way."*

Mr. Maxwell was dressed in a suit and tie and walked with purpose and with an air of authority. He would not be a person kids would want to cross based on the aura of professionalism he exuded. His demeanor was that of a no-nonsense kind of guy who couldn't be sucked into believing any of the students' fabrications and hallway drama, and yet he seemed quite approachable to students, even calling out some of their names as they loitered by their lockers or stood at the side doors leading to the parking lot, talking to some of their friends.

Mr. Maxwell led Mitch into a rather small, cluttered office of the gym and introduced him to Mr. Kaiser. Greg Kaiser stood up and shook Mitch's hand and pointed to a foldable chair on the other side of his desk.

"Nice to meet you, Mr. Neubauer. I've read a lot about you and consider you quite a hero."

"Thanks," replied Mitch humbly.

"I understand you've come to ask some questions about Andy Chandler regarding his father's murder. He played football for me about seven to nine years ago. He played his last three years of high school, so it's been a long time since I've seen him. I'm not sure I will be of much help, but ask away. What would you like to know?"

"Well, why don't you start off by telling me things you remember about Andy. What kind of kid was he?"

"Oh, Andy was a nice enough kid. He didn't have a mouth on him. He was more of a follower than a leader. Never caused any trouble. He didn't have a great athletic ability. Sometimes I wondered why he even tried out for the team. He didn't seem to enjoy playing the game, never seemed to quite grasp the plays or even the basic concepts of the game."

"So was he slow academically?" inquired Mitch.

"No, I don't think so. He just never put out, if you know what I mean. He wasn't an ambitious or energetic kid. He lacked curiosity and motivation."

"So why do you think he tried out for the team every year?"

"Oh, he probably thought being on the team would make him popular or get the girls, but he benched it most of the time."

"Was he popular?"

"Not that I could tell."

"Was he a likable kid?"

"Yes, I guess you could say he was a nice boy. Clean cut and all, but he was lazy and had a sense of entitlement about him that always bugged me."

"Why was that?" Mitch asked with a curious tone.

"I guess because his dad and stepfather were both rich, and he thought that somehow made him special."

"Did you ever meet Mr. Chandler, Mr. Kaiser?"

"Actually, I did. Several times. He came to all of Andy's games—even though Andy seldom played."

"Well, did he ever complain to you about not playing his son enough?"

"No, he didn't. Mr. Chandler even came to some of the practices. Apparently he played high school and college football and saw clearly that Andy didn't get his athletic gene. He also saw his son not giving 100 percent in practice. We were lucky to get 50 percent out of Andy.

"Now Andy's mother tried to apply pressure on me to play him more. She was quite persistent and even got aggressive with me. It wasn't until she insinuated she would go to the superintendent about me if need be that I went off on her. I figured she would definitely report me to my superiors and she did. Mr. Maxwell called me into a meeting over it."

"And how did that go?"

"Let's just say we both had her number. I was left with no worries or concerns about Mrs. Darrington. The woman tried to flaunt her power and even get me fired, but no one was smitten by her wealthy demeanor or airs. Andy's pushy mom couldn't provide a good defense for playing her son more."

"So what were your thoughts about Mr. Chandler?"

"Well, he seemed like a very nice, unpretentious father who cared a lot about his son. I felt he was very knowledgeable about the game, respected the judgments and authority of me as a coach, and just wished his son was trying harder."

"Did you ever hear Mr. Chandler denigrate his son while he was sitting or standing on the sidelines?"

"No. He really seemed like a genuine nice guy. I can't say the same about his ex-wife."

"Did you ever hear Andy talk about his dad?"

"No, never. In fact, I remember seeing him totally ignoring his father who waited on the sidelines long after a practice or game to speak with Andy, but he never even walked over to talk to him. He never even made eye contact with him. I thought it strange."

"Did you ever ask Andy why he didn't talk to his dad?"

"In a round about way. I mentioned I had spoken to his father a few times and found him to be a caring parent. Andy did say, 'You don't know him' or something to that affect and walked away. Clearly he didn't want to talk about him, so I dropped it."

"One final question, and I won't keep you. I know you have another meeting to attend. I know you know Andy's dad and stepmother were murdered sometime back."

"Yes, I figured that's why you were here. I hope Andy isn't a suspect."

"Do you think it possible that Andy killed them, knowing what you know about Andy?"

"Absolutely not! We have had our share of ruffians at this school over the years—kids who have been in trouble with the law and it came as no surprise, but Andy was a kid who kept his nose clean. He didn't excel in our building academically or in sports, and he wasn't that well known. He was just an average kid who had a few friends and didn't leave our hallowed halls with a good or bad mark. He didn't show an aggressive bone in his body in football, so I can't imagine him killing anyone. Is he a serious suspect in this case, Mr. Neubauer?"

"The case is unsolved so far, so everyone, I guess you could say, who knew the Chandlers are suspects. I'd appreciate it if you would keep our meeting confidential, Mr. Kaiser, until this case has been solved. If you think of anything you feel is important for me to know about Andy Chandler or his mother or dad, please give me a call." And with that Mitch handed him his business card.

"I thank you for your time and, now, if you could direct me to Katherine Vargo's classroom, I would appreciate it."

CHAPTER 51

Mitch Neubauer was directed to Room 12 where Mrs. Vargo, Andy's former English teacher, was waiting for him. The room was decorated with many colorful wall posters that taught literary terms. Two bulletin boards displayed covers of books to encourage reading, both the classics and contemporary authors.

Mrs. Vargo didn't look much differently than his high school English teacher in the 90's. She was meticulously dressed in a navy blue and white pantsuit and navy pumps to match. She was a seasoned teacher, perhaps in her late forties and greeted him with a warm, welcoming smile. He liked her immediately.

"It's a pleasure to meet you, Mr. Neubauer. I surely hope Andy isn't a suspect in the murders of his father and stepmother." Mrs. Vargo knew how to cut to the chase, probably from reading a lot of suspense novels Mitch thought.

"Well, if you've kept up on the news, you know the case has not been solved so everyone who ever knew the Chandlers is technically a suspect," replied Mitch.

"I see," she said with some sadness. *"So what do you want to know?"*

"Can you share your observations about Andy when he was in your class?"

"Well, it's been about seven years since I had him. He was in my senior English class and in my senior study hall. He was a polite young

man. He never gave me one day of trouble. I liked him a lot, but I felt kind of sorry for him."

"Why was that, Mrs. Vargo?" Mitch asked.

"Oh, I don't know. He never really seemed happy. He never laughed like the other kids did. He seldom even smiled. He looked kind of sad to me."

"Why do you think that was?"

"Well, I'm not a psychologist, but I know Andy hated school by his own admission. He missed a lot of his homework assignments and would do bare minimum work. He didn't like studying or anything that required him to sit and listen or take notes. He never utilized his time in Study Hall either so he could get his work done.

"He did like going to movies. He used to tell me all the movies he saw over the weekend. He just never thrived in school."

"Did he have a learning disability that you were aware of?"

"No. I think he was just kind of lazy and unmotivated. And he was definitely spoiled," she added.

"How so?"

"He always wore brandname clothes and had a cell phone, an iPod, and every other electronic gadget known to man."

"Did he ever write anything in, let's say a composition, that raised any red flags for you?" Mitch asked.

"Like what?"

"Like his feelings toward his family or friends."

"Not that I can recall. If he had, I probably would have remembered that. I turn papers of concern usually over to a counselor to assess whether the student needs intervention—like suicidal thoughts or expressions for hurting someone. No, Andy was a sweet kid.

"Not every kid who walks through our hallowed halls, Mr. Neubauer, is going to like school. Andy probably would have been more successful had he attended a vocational school where he could be in a lab much of the day with hands-on training."

"Had you met Andy's parents?"

"Yes, I met his mother on a number of occasions. Whenever Andy would get a poor grade on a progress report or a report card, Mrs. Darrington usually called to see what was going on."

"So she was a supportive mother?"

"I'm not sure I would go quite that far. She implied, in a subtle way, that my educational standards in the classroom were too hard for the students and that I gave them too much work. It was always someone else's fault why Andy wasn't succeeding.

"I asked Mrs. Darrington if she saw Andy working on his assignments in the evening or writing his papers for class. She conceded that she had not even seen him bring any of his textbooks home, but he convinced her he had completed all of his work in his study halls. I assured her he was not utilizing his time in my study hall as he should be.

"When she had no answer for Andy's dereliction of duty, she intimated that she would need to speak to the principal about me because clearly there must be a personality conflict between her son and me. According to her, Andy was doing fine in all of his other classes except for English. I checked on that, however, and learned that Andy was earning below average grades in most of his courses, not just mine. Mrs. Darrington had had similar conversations with the other teachers as well, so she tried to strong arm all of us into showing some undeserved mercy to her lazy but quite capable son. So you could say that Mrs. Darrington and I were not endeared to each other."

"Do you remember Mr. and Mrs. Chandler at all?"

"Yes, actually I do. After their pictures were shown in the newspaper—after their murders—I remembered them well.

"They seemed like a very nice couple, truly concerned about Andy. They made no excuses for his disinterest in school, and yet were quite disappointed he wasn't utilizing his abilities. They both were very supportive of us teachers. They admitted that they had little influence over Andy as non-custodial parents, but they would do what they could to see his grades improve.

"Without their actually verbalizing it in so many words, I could tell by their body language and a few things Mr. Chandler said that he didn't *see eye to eye with Mrs. Darrington about Andy's house rules, discipline, values system and personal freedoms, but his hands were tied. He was still holding on, though, trying to be a responsible father."*

"Any impressions about the new Mrs. Chandler?"

"The fact that she came along being a teacher herself and having evening work to do showed me she took a genuine interest in Andy. The Chandlers struck me as a very nice, loving, caring couple. I just didn't get the same feeling with the snooty Mrs. D."

"Well, thanks for the insights, Mrs. Vargo. So in summation, you feel Andy definitely had the ability to do your work but was just unmotivated and unwilling to do it, and that his mother was trying to find an easy escape for Andy through coercion with teachers."

"Yes, that would sum it up in a kind way."

"Thanks, Mrs. Vargo. Here is my business card. If there's anything else you might think would be important or shed light on this case, feel free to call me."

On Mitch's way out of her room, he turned to Mrs. Vargo.

"One last question. Do you think it likely that Andy had anything to do with the killing of his father and stepmother?"

"No, not really. Andy could get a little sarcastic when I confronted him when he was wasting his time in Study Hall, but he was a rather passive teen. Good luck with your investigation, Mr. Neubauer. I hope you find the person who killed the Chandlers."

CHAPTER 52

Mitch walked up a flight of stairs in search of Room 200. George Grover, Andy's former math teacher, was sitting at his desk, grading papers. He politely rose from his seat as soon as Mitch entered the room.

"Mr. Neubauer?"

"Yes, hello."

"Come in. Nice to meet you. Have a seat right here." Mr. Grover offered him a chair used at his personal computer table. Mitch shook Mr. Grover's hand and sat down.

"You probably know I'm here about the double homicide of Andy Chandler's father and stepmother."

"Yes, Mr. Maxwell indicated that was your purpose. I doubt that I would know anything that could illumine you on the case, however. I met the Chandlers several times here in the building but never made a parent/teacher call at their house. What sort of things do you want to know? I surely hope Andy isn't a suspect."

"We have no evidence to point to that, but certainly since the case hasn't been solved, anyone who knew the Chandlers is technically a suspect."

"Sure. Well, okay. Ask away."

"What can you tell me about Andy as a person and as a student?"

"Well, if you don't mind me being totally blunt, he stood out as one of the laziest kids I ever had in class and yet he had as much ability as any other student I ever had. He liked to sleep in my class and put forth zero effort."

By now Mitch wasn't surprised to hear that. Every teacher was pretty consistent with the word *lazy* when describing Andy.

"Andy was never willing to stay after school to be tutored, so he wasn't willing to help himself. He was apathetic. He didn't seem to care if he passed or failed until the week before grade cards came out.

"I'm sure he copied the answers to his homework off other students' papers, which helped him get by. I also believe he cheated on my tests. He was devious even though he was a likable kid. He was, nevertheless, a sneak and I didn't trust him."

"Did you actually catch him cheating?"

"Oh, yeah. Numerous times. He had mathematical formulas written out in the palm of his hand. He didn't know it but once I alternated student tests. He and the kid next to him who I figured was his partner in crime had the same exact answers on their tests and yet they had two very different versions. They were shocked when they got caught red handed, so they had to devise different cheating techniques. I had to stay a step ahead of him and his circle of cheating friends."

Mr. Grocer laughed as he relived those moments.

"But then it didn't take long for his mother to come in and see me. Or should I say threaten me," Grover continued.

"She threatened you?"

"She told me her son had studied for two hours for that math test and was so befuddled that I had asked questions over material not ever covered in class—which was a lie—that he got so frustrated, he resorted to cheating that time on the test. She demanded I let her son retake the test. I refused. No student in my class is going to get rewarded for cheating on a test.

"When I told her that her son had cheated on other tests as well and on homework assignments, she proceeded to accuse me of spending

more time trying to weed out class cheaters than to teach math. She had an answer for everything. She said that a number of parents and students were unhappy with my teaching ability, and she planned to go before the board and have me terminated."

"Were the parents and students unhappy?"

"No. I knew she couldn't back up what she was saying, but she was intimidating for sure. She could and would cause trouble for me. She isn't a person you'd want to have as an enemy."

Both Mitch and Grover looked at each other for a minute as they meditated on the depth of that statement.

"So did she cause trouble for you as promised?"

"She certainly did take her complaints to the board, and the assistant principal began scrutinizing my lesson plans carefully for weeks and stopped by my classroom frequently while I was up front teaching. It was under the pretense of looking for a particular student needed down in the office for a disciplinary action, but I knew why he was really there. He was trying to placate Mrs. Darrington. Since students were never taken out of my class and sent to the office, it was obvious he was collecting enough proof to defend me should Mrs. D. carry her complaint further."

"And did she?"

"No. Nothing was going to appease her until I was fired, but by then the school knew Mrs. Darrington for what she was."

"And what was she?" asked Mitch.

"She was a woman who thought she had clout because she had money. Her famous line was, 'You have no idea who you're dealing with.'"

"So I assume you weren't on her Christmas card list?" asked Mitch with a smile.

"Hardly," Mr. Grover replied sarcastically. *"I hate to say this, but it's too bad Mrs. D. wasn't the one who was murdered rather than Andy's dad and stepmom. Now they were nice folks."*

"So you knew the Chandlers?"

"*Yes. Well, I knew Ivy because she taught high school math too and we took some continuing education classes in the summer together. That's actually how I met her. I knew her long before she became Mrs. Chandler.*"

"*What was she like?*"

"*She was funny and enthusiastic and just a genuinely sweet lady. Everyone liked Ivy,*" Grover said factually.

"*Unfortunately, there was someone who didn't, Mr. Grover.*"

"*Did Andy know you knew his stepmother?*"

"*Yes, and he avoided talking about her everytime I asked about her.*"

"*What would he say?*"

"*He said, 'You know her as a colleague. I know her as a stepmother. Two very different things.' He would never elaborate about those comments, but he clearly didn't like her.*"

"*Did he dislike her enough to kill her or have her killed?*"

"*Oh, I don't think so!*" Grover answered adamantly. "*I can't imagine. Kids either like math or they don't. There's usually no in-between. Kids who don't like math sometimes cheat. That's school, Mr. Neubauer, but when kids speak ill of a parent or stepparent – sometimes out of frustration— that doesn't make them murderers.*"

"*Just askin', Mr. Grover.*"

"*I do know he thought Ivy was too strict and picky, and it was his dad's house. In his mind she had no right to tell him what to do when the dad was there. That's probably just a natural rebellion that most kids from divorced homes experience.*"

"*The only difference is, the parents of those kids don't end up dead.*"

CHAPTER 53

Mitch returned to the front office and had to wait for Mr. Maxwell to finish a phone call before being ushered in to his office. His office was rather small but comfortable. He had a few family pictures on the credenza behind his desk. Mitch was drawn to a picture of Maxwell and his wife with what looked to be their twin sons of maybe thirteen or fourteen years of age.

"Have a seat, Mr. Neubauer. Were the teachers you met able to help you?"

"Well, they gave me some important insights into Andy. Thank you."

"Good. Good. Well, I've pulled Andy's discipline record out for you as you requested. It's a small file and a short read. As I told you, Andy was never a discipline problem in this school. His attendance for his final four years was good. He had several after school detentions for the dastardly deed of sleeping in class."

Of course Mitch could tell Mr. Maxwell was being facetious.

"He was suspended for three days for participating in a fight."

"A fight?" Mitch asked curiously.

"My notes indicate he was in a class with a substitute teacher on that day. The teacher had stepped into the hallway for a minute and when she stepped back into the room, Andy was engaged in a physical fight with another young man in class. No one was hurt, but our school policy is that no matter who provoked or started the fight, if the other party fights back, both get suspended."

"It isn't always justice, Mr. Neubauer, but it is impossible to distinguish the truth of what and who started it all. What I have recorded about this incident is Andy's version. He told me that a particular kid had been making derogatory comments about him since the first day of school and had continued bullying him in class. When the teacher left the room, the bully got out of his seat and got Andy in a choke hold so that he couldn't breathe. Andy had no other choice but to fight.

"I had a long, private talk with Andy. He had been bullied by kids since kindergarten, according to him. He normally ignored it, but when the kid grabbed him at the throat from behind, he had had enough. It was time to retaliate. So he fought back with all he had.

"I remember I had quite a heart to heart with Andy that day. He let his guard down and we had what I would call almost a father-son talk. He shared some very personal, inner feelings with me that I doubt he had shared with anyone ever before. In fact, he shed a few tears and was embarrassed by it, but I saw a boy who was hurting inside. He was much more sensitive than he ever let show."

"So what do you think was the underlying pain he was carrying around?"

"I think he felt he was never accepted by anyone. He wasn't successful at sports, in his academic classes or with the girls, and didn't seem to be happy in his personal life either, although he never got into that with me. But clearly he made some innuendos to imply that. I had a few encounters with his mother, Mrs. Darrington, and she was memorable, to say the least. Something was locked up inside that kid. I could see a genuinely sweet and tender kid. He had a good heart. I liked Andy, and I felt sorry for him. Still, I had no other choice but to give him a three day suspension. I think Andy was okay with that. He knew it was coming, but I think our friendly conversation was meaningful to him."

Mitch thanked Mr. Maxwell for his time and headed for the door to the parking lot. The words *something was locked up inside that kid* kept bothering Mitch. What was locked up inside him? Mitch also liked Maxwell. He wished he had had a Mr. Maxwell for a principal when he was in high school. Mitch's dad had died when he was nine years old, and he needed someone at school that he could unabashedly confide in and bare his soul to. Andy seemed to be his mother's pawn in the divorce. A kid could lose his sense of belonging and perhaps even his identity going back and forth from home to home. Lots of kids in our nation have to live that way. It's not uncommon. Many manage to get through it okay. The question is, Did this boy Andy Chandler who everyone agreed was a nice boy get through it okay? As a father of two sons himself, Mitch was hoping Andy was innocent.

A small piece of paper had been wedged under the windshield of Mitch's Buick Lacrosse. He carefully pulled it out while quickly looking around the parking lot for the author, but no one was in sight. He began reading the typed note:

Mrs. Darrington is a mean, sly, nasty bitch! She's the likely candidate for the Chandlers' murders.

CHAPTER 54

B arnabus had been prepped for his meeting with Rita Darrington. He had all of the confirmed background information on her. He knew everything that was in her past divorce decree and all of the arrangements for child support and child visitation. He had been provided all of the court records—the reason for being in court, who filed, and the outcomes—by Jean, their very efficient secretary. He had a record of every one of Bill Chandler's payments to the Summit County Child Support Enforcement Agency, dated. Jean even checked police records for domestic violations against Bill by either Rita or Ivy. There were none. So Barnabus had all of the proven facts prior to meeting Andy Chandler's mother.

He also knew that early on in this homicide case, the police were able to verify Rita and Chaz's alibi on the evening of the murders. That would prove they didn't kill the Chandlers, but it didn't prove they didn't hire someone to do it for them.

From the assessment of so many people who had crossed paths with Rita Marie Morgan Darrington, she was a very vindictive person who demanded retribution from anyone she felt crossed her in some way. Accounts had to be settled, so in her narcissistic way of thinking, did she hold Bill and Ivy accountable for an internalized wrong?

Doug sent Barnabus to the Darrington home to apply pressure to Rita, hoping she might panic and say things pertinent to the case that would point to the responsible person for the Chandler murders—if she knew, that is.

Barnabus had made the appointment for 10:00 a.m. He wore a black suit, a crisp white shirt underneath, and a red striped power tie. Barnabus drove his black Miata up their long, winding driveway. The front yard was large, well manicured with a three tiered courtyard fountain. The house was opulent.

Rita opened the door before he had time to knock. He immediately showed her his identification badge. Her face was stoic, and he could see she looked a little intimidated by him. He wasn't sure if it was because of his size, his professional demeanor, or the reason for which he had come. Whatever it was, she looked uncomfortable and edgy, and Barnabus liked that. It gave him an immediate advantage.

Rita led him into the family room. He chose the carved arm chair. As he looked around, he was quite surprised at how plebeian the interior of the house was decorated compared to the outside of the house. It was decorated rather cheaply with drab colors.

Barnabus explained that their investigative company had been hired by Helen Porter and Alayna Fisher, Ivy's mother and sister.

"Yes, I know who they are," Rita responded rather sardonically. *"I'm very sorry for their loss, but I had nothing to do with the murders and my alibi has been verified, so I'm not sure why you're here. I hadn't seen nor heard from my ex-husband in over seven or eight years prior to his death. We weren't really on speaking terms after the divorce, as I'm sure you're already aware of."*

"I guess most divorces aren't all that friendly or couples wouldn't be divorcing in the first place, right?" Barnabus asked, trying to find common ground with Rita and win over her trust.

"You can say that again," she quickly responded, but Barnabus could tell she was trying to anticipate where he was going with all of this.

Barnabus had been well trained in interrogation techniques, so no matter how alert she was, Rita wouldn't be able to prepare herself for the direction this interview would take her.

"Do you have any thoughts on who may have wanted to kill your ex-husband or his wife?" Barnabus asked.

"None whatsoever. I've already shared this with the police. I only met Ivy a few times, so I can't say as I knew her at all."

"I see," said Barnabus. *"Are there any occasions you can recall when there was friction between the two of you?"*

"No, but she was the creator of many problems I had with Bill."

"How do you mean?"

"Bill was allowed to have Andy for three weeks' vacation. After he married Ivy, he started asking for more."

"Didn't the divorce decree state that Bill could have Andy for three weeks with the possibility of five weeks?"

Rita realized Mr. Jones was educated on their divorce decree, so there wouldn't be any bluffing him.

"Well, yes it does, but Bill never wanted Andy for more until Ivy came along, and then he insisted on having him for half the summer."

"It was probably a good time for Ivy to bond with Andy and in the evenings when Bill would get home from work, he could have some quality time with Andy. Don't you think?" asked Barnabus sincerely.

Rita had a look of disgust on her face.

"No, I don't think that! He was tearing Andy away from playing with his friends and being with his family here."

"Bill and Ivy were his family also."

"They didn't care about Andy. They were just being punitive by trying to take Andy away from me and Chaz. Andy preferred being with us."

"Did Andy actually say that?"

"Yes. Yes, he did. Many times, in fact. Over at Bill's, he was an only child, but at our house, he had other siblings to play with.

"Besides, if Bill loved Andy so much, he would have been faithful in paying his child support. He wouldn't have forced me to take him to court for the money. Many times he was late paying it as well so we had to struggle financially until we got it," Rita said sadly.

179

"How many times did you have to take him to court for the child support?"

Barnabus asked even though he knew the answer.

"Too many to count," Rita responded factually.

"Hmmm. I actually looked through those payments and didn't see one late or missed payment in those fifteen years. Not one."

"His child support was garnished from his own company—a company he owned and controlled, Mr. Johnson. Down to the very last dollar. He can make all of his accounts look flawless.

"I didn't want to take Bill to court over all of those things. I certainly didn't have the financial means to fight him until I married Chaz, but my son was getting cheated out of what his dad owed him, and I wasn't about to let his deadbeat dad cheat him out of that!" The anger on her face could not be hidden.

"Bill was supposed to pay for Andy's health insurance, and I had to go after him for that too."

"So were there a lot of those?"

"Oh, yes! Andy needed braces and later a retainer, which he lost twice. Then he needed glasses, and he accidentally lost those twice. Bill needed to replace those and got angry about that. He actually refused, forcing me to take him to court again. Then Andy was diagnosed early on with ADD (attention deficit disorder) and later with exercise-induced asthma, and the list goes on."

"Did you work, Mrs. Darrington?"

"I worked when Bill and I were married, but when we got divorced, I was forced to stay home and take care of Andy. My money supply had pretty much ended."

"Did you get any alimony?"

"Well, yes. A little."

"If I recall correctly from court records, you were receiving $3,000 a month until you remarried, which was how long after the divorce?"

Barnabus asked, knowing the answer to that question as well.

Rita squinted her eyes and gave Barnabus a contemptible look. She knew he was making a point, and she resented it.

"I don't recall. It was quite some time later," she lied. She knew precisely the answer to those questions.

"Three thousand dollars sounds pretty good to me, Mrs. Darrington. My mother only got $250 a month for me when Dad left us."

"Bill could well afford it. Trust me. He worked his tail off getting his business up and running. In fact, that's all he thought about was his company and those damn boxes! He ignored me and Andy in those days."

Barnabus knew he had hit a nerve.

"So he was struggling to build a successful company in your earlier years together, finally making a decent living when you parted."

"Yes. That's pretty accurate."

"So with the alimony and child support, you no longer needed to work, weren't required back then to pay half of your son's living expenses, and then you remarried."

"When Bill didn't come through with his child support, I certainly had to support my son."

"I'll have to go back and retrace that, Mrs. Darrington. I couldn't find one court record showing you taking Mr. Chandler to court for delinquent payment of child support nor did I find a record showing checks sent late."

Mrs. Darrington looked smug but didn't say a word.

"I didn't want a divorce, Mr. Johnson. Really, I didn't. My husband ignored Andy and me the entire five years we lived together as a family. Bill may have been stressed over the struggling company, but he was very abusive to me!"

"In what way, Mrs. Darrington?"

"He yelled at me constantly. He was a tightwad and became angry with my spending of our money. He deliberately tried to make me feel inferior. He was emotionally abusive as well. He never met my needs physically, emotionally, socially, or any other way."

"When you divorced, I understand that you got the BMW. Is that correct?" Barnabus asked innocently.

"It was MY car anyway! Bill bought it for me. It was titled in my name."

"According to Helen Porter, Bill sent your parents to Hawaii for their 40th or 50th wedding anniversary. Is that true?"

"WE sent them. I worked too."

"Right. You worked as a secretary at Chandler Corbox. Is that correct?"

"Yes. I was paid well. I have a business degree . . ."

"Yes, it was an Associates degree in secretarial studies, as I recall. Is that correct?"

Barnabus could see Rita's agitation building up.

"Yes, that's correct."

"And, I believe, Helen Porter told us that Bill had given you, your Mom and Dad Rolex watches one year for Christmas. Is that correct?"

"Yes. That was Bill's way of saying he was sorry for the way he treated me. He had been physically abusive to me and was afraid I would go to the police."

"You didn't?"

"No, but I should have."

"Did your folks know Bill was physically abusive to you?"

"I told them eventually. I believe we were separating then."

"But you never confided in them prior to that time?"

"No. I told some of my closest friends, but I didn't want my folks to dislike Bill or there be an altercation between my dad and him."

"How many times would you say Bill physically harmed you?"

"Too many," Rita said cautiously.

"Did you call the police and report any of these incidents?"

"No. I don't know why I didn't. I just decided to leave Bill and get away from him.

"Did any of your injuries require medical attention?"

"No. He slapped me, twisted my arm, shoved me into the wall. Those kinds of things." The poignant look on her face was desperately seeking his sympathy.

"Did Andy witness any of these physical altercations?"

"No. Bill was discreet. He made sure Andy was in another room or sleeping," Rita said while tears welled up in her eyes. She was not only a pathological liar but a superb actress, thought Barnabus. She was so delusional, it appeared even she was believing her lies.

"Did Andy ever witness Bill getting angry with you or yelling at you?"

"Of course he did. I'm sure of that. But Andy was so young, he would have no recollection of them anyway.

"Andy knew later why I got the divorce. Kids get curious about those things. It was Andy's right to know the truth when he got older and inquisitive."

"Just a few more questions, Mrs. Darrington. These are more about Andy. How did he handle the divorce?"

"He adapted quite well. He was so young after all. He was only four years old."

"The visitation with Bill and Ivy ended a little short. Do you know why?"

"Andy hated how his father had treated me over the years. Andy was quite protective of me. Bill hurt me, and I guess, it hurt Andy. You try to protect your child from much of the pain, but kids pick up on things. They eavesdrop on phone conversations. They know more than we think they do.

"Bill never spent a lot of money on Andy when he had the weekend and midweek visitations, and he and Ivy limited Andy's TV watching and computer game play time. Our homes are run very differently. When Andy would return to our home after a visitation, we would review how he spent his time there. I have to agree with Andy, I wouldn't want to be there either. It wasn't a kid friendly environment."

"So the values system was much different," commented Barnabus.

"Night and day different," said Rita with a smile.

"Does that make them wrong or just different?" asked Barnabus.

"In my opinion as Andy's mother and the ex-wife to Bill—wrong!"

"Do you recognize the term 'Ivy Connivy'?"

Rita smirked.

"Oh, that was nothing. It was a harmless term we used occasionally when Ivy would do something to annoy us."

"Did Andy call her that too?"

"Only in our home. As I said, it was harmless."

"May I ask why Andy never went to college? After all, he certainly should have had the money to go, didn't he?"

"Andy had no desire to go. He was an average student. He went through school mostly with untreated ADD, thanks to his dad, so he couldn't concentrate or stay focused on his classes. That probably had a lot to do with it. So his dad indirectly restricted the career direction Andy could go."

"Could you and Mr. Darrington have afforded to buy Andy's medicine for the ADD?" Barnabus asked.

Rita chafed at the suggestion and the implication.

We did everything for Andy, but there are some things his own dad was expected to do for him. And when he didn't, we knew Andy would come to his own conclusions that his dad didn't meet his responsibilities and probably never loved him. The truth hurts, but Andy knew Chaz and I loved him, and we would always be there to be his safety net."

"So Andy felt his dad didn't love him and had cheated him out of what he owed him?"

"Sure, he did, because it's true! I told Andy his dad was so frugal he would probably never get a dime out of his father after he turn eighteen, and he didn't!"

"But by then, hadn't Andy estranged himself from Bill and Ivy?"

"Yes, but you never stop being a father, do you? Well, Bill did! Here he was now filthy rich, living the good life, and he never once sent Andy a check in his birthday or Christmas card. Never offered to help him out when Andy could have used some help starting out in life.

"Well, I feel bad that Bill was murdered, but none of us really miss him. Least of all Andy," she remarked.

"I hope those feelings aren't what's brought us here today, Mrs. Darrington."

"I assure you they didn't, Mr. Johnson," she said with such confidence.

With that, Barnabus stood up, shook her hand and walked toward the front door. As he walked to his Miata, he could see the kind of controlled dynamics and brainwashing that went on in that home.

If Barnabus hadn't known the facts prior to coming here, he would have been prone to believe Mrs. Darrington. She was quite convincing in the way she told her stories. He also knew that almost nothing of what she had told him had any veracity whatsoever.

Had she told these lies so many times that she actually believed them herself? It wasn't that she was embellishing some truths; there was no evidence there was even one remnant of truth to her stories. As his mother would have said, *She was pure evil!*

In Barnabus's mind, Rita Darrington was a very dangerous lady and mother. She had done a great injustice to her son by feeding him lies about his father. Bad feelings about Andy were springing up from within, and he was hoping his hunch was wrong, for he really liked Andy.

CHAPTER 55

Doug Conrad called a meeting with his team to discuss each member's findings regarding the Chandler case. Doug had promised Ivy's mom and sister that he would keep them updated on their progress, and they had assured him they would be available to answer any questions for them that might come up.

Mitch had provided a summary of the teachers' assessments of Andy Chandler while as a junior and senior at Ellet High School. He also mentioned the interesting note left on his windshield suggesting Mrs. Darrington's involvement in the murders. Of course, it contained no substance or proof, but it did speak to Mrs. Darrington's character and her reputation among the faculty members. The most interesting notation was that Andy had a sneaky side to him, but he was a young man that was hurting inside and very unhappy but just never showed it on the outside. *"Something was locked up inside that kid,"* as the principal put it.

Donna Gifford began summarizing her encounter with Wendy Graves. A few important things were obtained from their conversation: Rita was very open about stating that Bill Chandler got what he deserved. A rather callous statement. Rita told Wendy that Bill was *"meaner than a snake."* Andy never mentioned his dad ever mistreating him, but he was quite aware of Bill mistreating the mother. He definitely didn't like Ivy. Andy dropped by the Bacher Funeral Home during visiting hours—seemed unmoved, left quickly as he felt uncomfortable around the other family members. He never shared with Wendy any bad experience he had in the Chandler home during his visitations, so she didn't sense Andy had ever been mistreated. Donna had suggested Wendy dig a little deeper with Andy concerning some of those family issues. Donna planned to return to Macy's to speak with Wendy again under the guise, of course, of shopping for a gift.

Then Zap began to share his experience at the gym with Andy. Andy was extremely reticent to mention his dad and stepmother were murdered. He stated he was at peace not knowing who killed them. He confessed he wasn't close to his father, and his stepmother was virtually a nonentity in his life. But then Andy left the gym and drove to his father and Ivy's house. Zap saw Andy pull into their driveway and lean over his steering wheel and appeared to be crying.

"So maybe it isn't the load that weighs us down as much as the way we carry it," said Doug.

Donna Gifford then shared her lengthy conversation with Rita at the hair salon. The three men were astounded by the many specific details Rita provided Donna on how to screw a divorced husband and father. The lady was devious! Rita's goal was clearly to put a deep abyss between the father and son. Again Rita detailed for all the ladies in the salon how she had been physically, mentally, verbally, and emotionally abused by Bill Chandler. *"She was so credible and visual in the telling of her story*, said Donna, *that she had earned all of the women's sympathy.* Rita suggested that the murderer was either a provoked student of Ivy's or an enemy that Bill had made.

Rita's final thought was that when all of the dust settles, Andy would inherit most of Bill's estate and personal worth. So she had been thinking about the good that could come to Andy from Bill's and Ivy's deaths.

As Donna tried to pull all of this information together, her inference was that Rita probably wasn't involved in the murders, but because of her rearing techniques, she may have been totally responsible for the deaths of these two people.

"My mother used to tell me, 'it is easier to leave angry words unspoken than to mend a heart those words have broken,'" said Doug. *"I wonder*

if Mrs. Darrington has any clue of the damage her lies about Andy's dad may have done to her son. I hope and pray Andy had nothing to do with these two homicides, but if he did, Mrs. Darrington will need to reconcile in her own mind her role in all of that. Ah, the insight of hindsight."

Doug decided it was now time for him to meet Andy Chandler.

CHAPTER 56

Doug was scheduled to meet with Andy Chandler at Andy's apartment at 6 p.m. Doug didn't have time to eat dinner, so he stopped by Strickland's ice cream parlor on Triplett Boulevard near the Harding Square Apartments for a large chocolate custard. He and Cynthia used to go there often and then walk over to the Akron Municipal Airport to watch small airplanes take off and land. The memory seemed like a lifetime ago for Doug.

Doug finished his cone and drove to the circle and took a right onto Massillon Road and into the parking lot. Andy's apartment was on the first floor at the very end of the building. He knocked on Andy's door precisely at 6 p.m. Andy probably hadn't been home from work that long, for he still was in his work clothes, Docker pants and a dress shirt with an open collar. No tie.

"Andy Chandler? I'm Doug Conrad," said Doug in a very friendly tone as he held out his hand and his badge, identifying himself as a private investigator. *"I told you over the phone that I've been hired by Helen Porter and Alayna Fisher to investigate your father and stepmother's murders."*

"Yes, I know who you are. I recognize your name and face from the news. I'm really sorry about what happened to your family. Please, come in and have a seat."

Andy seemed very sincere and even compassionate. Doug liked him immediately.

The apartment was sparsely decorated. There was a small couch and one chair and a coffee table in the living room. There was a small 26 inch TV sitting on a small table across from the couch. A card table and two card table chairs were serving as a kitchen table in his very small kitchenette.

"Thank you. I appreciate it. Losing a loved one due to violence has been very difficult for me and my kids, so I think I know a little of what you are feeling."

He watched Andy's countenance after he made the remark, but Andy didn't nod his head in agreement or react in any way.

"So how are you doing with this, Andy?"

"I'm doing okay, Mr. Conrad. My circumstances were quite different from yours."

"In what way, son?" asked Doug sincerely and in his sweet fatherly tone.

"Well, you obviously had a very close knit, loving family. Mine wasn't like that, so I can't say I'm experiencing the same feelings you have."

"So how was your family?" asked Doug.

"My parents divorced when I was four. I have very few memories of my mom and dad ever living together in our home. I spent my childhood going back and forth from my Mom's house to my dad's."

"So many kids these days live in single parent homes and have to go back and forth, so it's quite common as you know. I guess it does get old."

"Yes, it did. I was glad when it was finally over."

"I understand you actually stopped visiting your dad shortly after you turned fifteen and earned your temporary car license. Is that correct?"

"Yes, I think so."

"Visitation continues until age 18 legally. Why did you stop visiting your dad?"

"That question sounds like I'm a suspect."

"Andy, the case is getting cold. It's been over one and a half months, and it still hasn't been solved. The longer it goes unsolved, the colder the

trail becomes. So I guess, in all honesty, anyone who was related, was a friend or even an acquaintance to your dad or Ivy would be considered a suspect. The more we learn about the victims and the family dynamics, the more helpful it will be in solving the case. The idea of a serial killer is being considered as well, so we're not leaving any rocks unturned."

Andy looked tense but made an attempt to look relaxed and not concerned.

"So back to my question. Were there problems between you and your father or Ivy?"

"No, not really. I was just getting more involved with my friends and school activities, and I was tired of being required to go see my dad."

"So was it an obligation to 'see him?'"

"Yes, it was. My dad pretended to love me, but he really didn't."

"Why do you think that?"

"Because he never wanted to pay his child support for me or any of my health bills. He begrudged having to pay. He was constantly arguing with my mother about the money, and yet he was swimming in money."

"Did you overhear some of the arguments between your parents over these issues?"

"No. They would talk on the phone apparently when I was at school. When I got old enough to understand things, my mom filled me in on that stuff. She was always having to take my dad to court to force him to pay. He was one of the deadbeat fathers you hear about all of the time. Meanwhile, my dad was spending money on himself and,

of course, on money hungry Ivy." Andy's tone was bitter and he made no attempt to hide it.

"I'd like to show you something, Andy, if I may." Doug reached down and pulled his attaché case closer to him and opened it up. He pulled out the child support records from the Summit County Child Support Bureau from the time of the Chandler's legal separation until Andy graduated from high school in June at age nineteen.

"Could we sit at your kitchen table where we can have more room to look at the spreadsheet?"

"Okay," Andy said with trepidation but curiosity. He wasn't sure what Mr. Conrad was about to show him, but he was feeling nervous and insecure.

"Here are the records Summit County provided of your father's payments for the entire time he was required to pay for your child support. His own company garnished his wages and sent the check to the board. They, then, are the ones who actually sent your mother the check. The system is set up that way for monitoring the non-custodial parent, making sure they are meeting their familial responsibilities. If they aren't, the parent is sent a letter of admonishment and if the money doesn't eventually come in, an arrest is made for dereliction of parental duty.

"Now, remember, these records are accurate and have come from the bureau itself. Look down these spreadsheets. You'll see one year's record per page. Do you see even one late payment?" Doug sat quietly as he watched Andy look at the records. Andy's face turned ashen.

"These records had to be tampered with. There are court records proving my mom took my dad to court for the money," Andy said defensively.

"These records have been cross-checked with Chandler Corbox records, and they are a perfect match, Andy. We have proof that your father never missed one payment the entire time you were a minor. Not even one."

Doug could tell Andy was having an almost impossible time processing this information. These were facts that couldn't be denied. Andy's lower lip began to quiver and tears welled up in his eyes but never came down his cheeks.

"The court records can prove that simply isn't true," said Andy.

"I also have records of all of the domestic court hearings between your mom and dad. You can look through these court dockets and see the summary lines which state the purpose for the hearings. Not one is over failure to receive child support for you, and only one is over some health bills. If you look through these, find Case 15, and it will clearly show you what that situation was all about."

Andy found the case and quietly read for nearly ten minutes in utter silence. His face looked troubled, and he was having a hard time holding back his emotions. Tears finally overflowed and came running down his cheeks.

In an almost inaudible whisper, Andy said, *"Why would my mother lie about that?"*

"I'm not sure, Andy, but you may want to look up parental alienation syndrome. It might provide some answers to your mother's own justification.

"I'm sorry that I had to be the one to share this information with you, Andy. I'm sure it is very hurtful to you and even comes as a shock. Your mother's and stepfather's alibi on the night of the murders proved they weren't the murderers. It doesn't mean they couldn't have hired it out, but we can't see a motive. Your alibi couldn't be proven, so would you just tell me again where you were on that night?"

"I stopped off at McDonald's for a carry-out after work before going home. I think the police found me on the camera driving through the McDonald's drive-thru to verify that. I came home and watched TV the entire evening, except I had fallen asleep most of the evening. I woke up around 11:00 p.m. and got up, showered, and went to bed. I didn't know anything about the murders until the next day."

"So you never talked to anyone on the phone that evening?"

"No. I was really tired that evening. I just wanted to relax."

"Your dad and stepmother had a security system in their home. Did you know what their security code was to get into the house?"

"No. They never shared it with me, and I never asked."

"Did you ever shoulder surf when they were taking it off or putting it on?"

"No, I didn't care what it was. It was never my home."

"Did you ever sit in the hot tub with your Dad and Ivy?"

"Sure. Lots of times when I was a kid."

"Did you know where the circuit breaker was in the basement?"

"No."

"Just for your information, Andy, and maybe for some consolation, we've been reading through Ivy's journals, and it is very clear that your

dad and she loved you very much and hated your estrangement. Ivy had no idea that she would be murdered and that her journal would become public. Journals are very private and personal. People are usually very honest in them. Perhaps after this case gets solved—and it will get solved, Andy—you can read through her journals. You would know the depth of love and concern they had for you. They were good folks who didn't deserve to die like that."

Doug took a long pause and smiled at Andy.

"Well, I appreciate the time you gave me, Andy. If there is anything I can do for you, or you think of anything that might help this case, please feel free to call me anytime.

From our investigative work, we have learned that your father was highly respected by his employees and peers. He was described as a very kind and caring person. We got almost the same feedback about Ivy too. She was well respected by her students and faculty and many friends. Their marriage was a good one, dedicated to helping others. You were luckier than you knew. I'm sure both Bill and Ivy would be very proud of you today. You seem to be a very fine young man."

"Thanks, Mr. Conrad. You take care."

They shook hands and Doug stepped out of the apartment and headed for his car. He knew his own kids so well and could read them like a book. Andy was a bit more perplexing, but Doug knew he lied about one of his questions. The circuit breaker. He did know where it was. Doug's *sixth* sense kicked in. His meeting with Andy would be the catalyst for either eliminating him as a suspect or . . .

CHAPTER 57

Doug Conrad returned home and was met at the door by Snuggles, the family Shih-tzu. He bent down and picked her up, and she smothered his face with licks. Now that Cynthia was gone, he realized the void that Snuggles was able to fill for him. He was glad he was able to at least share the house with someone—or something—although Snuggles had always been considered a *family member* by every member of the Conrad family. Cynthia loved their dog so much. Until one has loved an animal, a part of one's soul remains unawakened. People who've never had a pet can't realize an animal's value.

Doug was so tired. He peeked inside the nearly empty refrigerator and decided to nuke a leftover from Bistro's. He turned the TV on but nothing excited him. He put his dirty dishes in the dishwasher and went upstairs to take a shower.

While basking under the hot water, Doug kept thinking about what a wonderful mother Cynthia was to Paul and Taylor. Everything Cynthia ever did for them was in their best interest. They trusted Cynthia explicitly. If she told them something, they knew it had to be true. Most kids would believe their mother. After all, why would a mother lie? It would be so disconcerting to learn your mother lied to you your entire life so that you would love her and disrespect the father. A child would feel so deceived.

So if a son had been told his father had done so many bad things to the mother he had loved and trusted for twenty-five years and he thought he had been mistreated indirectly by his father, would he hate the father enough to kill him? Could the mother have gotten her son so upset about the unfairness of being cheated out of his dad's wealth that he would want to simply take it all away from him?

Doug dried off and put a clean tee shirt on and his pajama bottoms. When he stepped into his bedroom, Snuggles had already come upstairs and was positioned on Cynthia's pillow, looking like she was waiting for Cynthia to step into the room at any moment. *A dog is faithful to the last beat of its heart*, thought Doug.

Doug was feeling rather melancholy. Cynthia wasn't coming back. Snuggles had sensed it also. The house was empty. Doug missed his kids and their banter, and now he was thinking about a nice young man just a little older than Paul who may have made the most serious mistake of his life because he had been duped by his mother for most of it. He hoped and prayed he was wrong. He would have trouble sleeping tonight.

CHAPTER 58

Donna Gifford returned to Macy's and took the escalator straight up to the Housewares Department. There were no shoppers in the department at the time. Donna had seen a KitchenAid mixer being advertised in the *Akron Beacon Journal* that she had been wanting. It was on sale and her mother's was so old, so it was time for a replacement. She would pretend, however, that she was buying it as a wedding gift for her niece living in Germany.

Wendy was rearranging a display of Cuisinart pans when Donna walked up to her.

"*Hi. Do you remember me?*" asked Donna.

Wendy turned and looked at Donna. Then, with a look of recognition and a smile, replied, "*Yeah, I do. You came in a week or so ago looking for a wedding gift for a niece who was living in Europe somewhere.*"

"*That's right. Germany.*"

"*Well, did you find out what she needed?*"

"*I did. She could use a mixer, and I saw in the paper where the KitchenAid is on sale. I'd like to look at it, but I think that would be the most useful and perfect gift for her.*"

"*Oh, it would be. I have that on my wedding registry now and really hope I get one for our wedding.*"

"*That's right. You're getting married around Thanksgiving, right?*"

"*Yes. November 28th.*"

Together they began to walk over to the display of kitchen mixers.

"Yes. I remember you told me about your fiancé's parents being murdered."

"Well, it was his dad and stepmother. His mother is still living."

"Yes, that's right. So did you ever ask your fiancé about some of the things we talked about?"

"Yes. Actually, I did, but Andy got very upset with me."

"Really? What about?"

"Just talking about his deceased father upset him."

"Did you obtain any information that helped you learn more about your fiancé?"

"Well, he seemed quite resentful that his dad got to keep the house they were living in and he and his mom had to move out. He did share with a sense of gloating, however, that his mom pretty much stripped the house before leaving it, so Mr. Chandler wasn't left with much. Eight months later his mom married their former next door neighbor whom she had been confiding in for a long time about her marital problems. According to his mother, his dad was physically and emotionally abusive, but Andy never witnessed any of that. His dad and stepmom came to all of his sports games, but his mom wouldn't allow Andy to walk over to the bleachers to even speak to them. I kind of thought that was mean. Mr. Chandler had driven quite a distance to watch him play."

"Yes, it does seem mean."

"Andy said his dad and Ivy took him on some very nice vacations. I guess he didn't like his stepmother. She's the one who made him do some chores and had established some of the house rules, and he didn't like that at all. But he really resented his father because his mom had to take him to court to force him to pay his child support."

"It sounds like Andy had a pretty tough childhood."

"Yes, I think he did. There's one thing that kind of bothered me about all the stuff he was sharing with me."

"What was that?" asked Donna.

"His mother was very controlling. She told Andy mean things about his father while he was so young. It seems to me she was trying to

brainwash him and turn him against his father. As his mother, she knew she could influence him. He was like putty in her hands. The best I could tell, Andy's dad and stepmother seemed like pretty caring parents to him. I wished I could have known them."

"Well, I'm sure there are two sides to every story. Too bad Andy didn't get to know them as he was maturing and perhaps hear their version of what happened."

"That's true, but now he never will get to do that. I know now to never bring his parents up again—not for awhile anyway. Andy got terribly upset with me for bringing it up. It was definitely a hot topic!"

"Perhaps if the police make an arrest for their murders, it will bring closure for him, and he will later be able to talk about them, remembering the good times together."

"Yeah. I hope so. Well, here are the mixers."

Donna looked over the one on display and smiling looked up at Wendy and said,

"I'll buy one."

Wendy reached down and picked up a box that shared the same model and serial numbers as the mixer on display that Donna was looking at. Wendy escorted her over to the cash register and rang up the sale.

"Thanks so much, Wendy. It was so nice talking to you. Good luck with your fiancé. I hope everything works out for you."

"Thanks. I hope your niece enjoys her mixer!"

"Oh, I'm sure she will!"

CHAPTER 59

Barnabus was sitting at the health bar sipping a pomegranate blueberry drink after a vigorous workout when Andy Chandler walked into the exercise room. As he looked around the area to see which machines were available for use, he spotted Zap sitting at the bar.

Barnabus was sporting his Semper Fidelis (Always Faithful) Marine tee shirt, looking tired but relaxed. Andy waved to Zap and walked over to him.

"Hi! It looks like you just finished your workout."

"Yeah. I got started a little early this afternoon. I'm meeting a marine buddy of mine and we're going to do some target practicing at an indoor firing range this evening."

"Oh yeah? So what did you do in the Marines?" Andy asked with curiosity.

"Well, I was a master gunnery sergeant for awhile until one day that ended abruptly."

"What happened?"

"We were in a mountainous region in northeastern Afghanistan. There had been a lot of enemy fire going on as we— my fellow Marines along with other U.S. and Afghan soldiers were being ambushed. I was firing a heavy machine gun from the turret of a gun truck, but as I got out to rescue one of my wounded marines, there was an explosion. The

next thing I knew, I was looking up at a medic who welcomed me back to the world. I had suffered from ventricular tachycardia and . . ."

"*What's that?*" Andy asked.

"*I had a very fast heart rhythm with no effective pulse and was unconscious. So they used an AED on me and I . . ."*

"*What's that?*" Andy asked again.

"*An automated external defibrillator where they zap you to deliver a heart shock to restore a normal heart beat, so . . ."*

"*Oh, so that's how you earned the nickname Zap?*"

"*Actually, it is. They had zapped me more times than you're supposed to, but they decided to try one more time . . . and I'm alive today to tell it.*

"*Supposedly, I had killed seven insurgents and was able to provide cover that allowed some of my team to fight their way out of certain death. They attributed my efforts to saving eight U.S. marines and five Afghan soldiers, so it was a good day for us,*" Barnabus said humbly.

"*That's awesome.*"

"*You want to come shooting with us tonight?*" asked Barnabus.

"*No. I don't own a gun.*"

"*Never?*"

"*I've shot guns before but never owned one.*"

"*Oh, yeah. What have you shot?*"

"*Just a .38 special and a few smaller guns.*"

Barnabus observed Andy's purposeful ambiguity regarding the makes of his guns.

"*My dad—well, actually he's my stepdad—was a hunter. He used to set up a shooting range with targets out in a thick wooded area behind his house in Fairlawn.*"

"*So are you any good?*" Barnabus asked.

"*No. In fact, I stink. I can't hit a thing unless it's close up. Shooting's not my niche. I doubt I will ever put a gun in my hand again.*"

"*Well, I guess I can see your point after your folks were murdered.*"

"*I better get going before it gets too crowded and I have to wait to use the machines,*" said Andy looking rather uncomfortable.

"*Sure thing, man. Good to see you.*"

CHAPTER 60

Chaz Darrington arrived at Bravo's at Summit Mall ten minutes before Doug Conrad walked in for their meeting. He had already chugged down two martinis. Rita had been interviewed by Conrad and now he was asked to meet with him. Did Conrad not meet with them together because he thought he could find some discrepancies in their stories and try to pin the Chandler murders on them? Their alibis had already been legitimized and as far as he knew, they were not suspects. Rita felt that Doug was perhaps suspecting Andy. Her other suspicion was that maybe Doug thought Rita and Andy were in collusion and had something to do with it. Chaz knew he and Rita had nothing to do with the murders. They were as shocked and perplexed by their murders as anyone when they learned of them.

Chaz was almost 100% sure Andy didn't do it, even though he didn't have a rock solid alibi. He had known Andy since he was a baby. He and Amy had been good friends with their neighbors, the Chandlers. Chaz and Amy had two young children, so Amy and Rita took turns watching the kids on weekends when one of them had Saturday evening plans. Andy had always been a very quiet, passive child. He tended to cry when he was intimidated by the other children rather than resort to slapping or hitting. He never became physical, so it would be hard to fathom Andy doing something as extreme as murder. He had never even seen Andy throw a temper tantrum.

The first time Chaz had laid eyes on Rita, there was *chemistry.* In fact, he had an indescribable craving for her. It was purely lust. He sensed she felt the same way about him. Since their yards were separated by a shallow wood, he would drive by as she was at her mailbox retrieving her mail. They would have lengthy conversations. Eventually, the conversations became flirtatious. Then it escalated to meeting at out of the way coffee shops for lunch and then calling each other at work. They had an emotional affair that quickly moved into a physical one. Both felt justified in having a sexual relationship. After all, their partners were inadequate in meeting their emotional, physical, and social needs.

Chaz and Rita had always denied their affair to close friends and family members who were bold enough to verbalize their suspicions. By dropping innuendoes that Bill had been physically, emotionally, and verbally abusive to Rita throughout their entire marriage was certainly justification in the eyes of society for her getting a divorce. Chaz's story was that Amy was so involved with the kids, she never took time for Chaz. They simply drifted apart and when Rita was enduring her abuses and had no place to turn, she confided in Chaz.

Neither of them had any idea they were falling in love with each other. It was all so insidious and even took them by surprise. It made for a socially acceptable story to the kids, the family, and their friends, but it really was a fabrication that could never be disproved. So in case Conrad was going to dig into infidelity and look for a motive there, he would be able to stand firm on the story he and Rita had designed for themselves.

Conrad was escorted by a young hostess to a back booth where Chaz was waiting. Chaz never got up but reached out to shake his hand. Even though Doug always showed his identification badge, there had been so much publicity about Cynthia's murder, the abductions, and now the recent killing of Quinton Reed, it really wasn't necessary. Anyone watching the news and keeping up with the case would remember this one for a long, long time. Doug had become quite an icon by the media, although he did his best to avoid them and allow the case to stay in the past.

"Thanks for meeting me for lunch, Mr. Darrington," said Doug politely. *"My company was hired by Helen Porter and Alayna Fisher, as your wife probably told you. That would be Ivy's mother and sister."*

"Well, I really didn't know them. I've seen them from a distance at some of Andy's football and soccer games and other school events, of course, but I've never engaged in a conversation with them. I'm sure they want to see the perpetrators be arrested for the murders. We all do so that we—Andy especially—can get this behind us. So what's on your mind, Mr. Conrad?"

It was obvious Chaz Darrington was a very direct kind of guy and wanted to get this interview over with quickly.

"If the Chandlers weren't killed by a serial killer, then we believe the killer was someone who knew Bill and Ivy. Do you have any guesses who would want to kill Bill or Ivy or both?" asked Doug.

"I never had a conversation with Ivy, so I couldn't say who might want to kill her. I was Bill's neighbor for eight years. We were actually good friends. He seemed like a nice guy. Amy and I even attended his wedding to Rita and we became friends socially. Bill is a perfect example of knowing a person based on what you see on the outside but not really knowing what they're really like on the inside."

"What do you mean, Mr. Darrington?"

"Well, on the surface Bill seemed like a 'gentle spirit.' I never heard him say anything unkind or act rude to anyone—least of all Rita. But he was a Dr. Jekyll and a Mr. Hyde. I was shocked when Rita finally confided to me about Bill's irrational temper and bizarre behavior. He was mean spirited, actually, and confrontational to Rita. He was accusatory and jealous. Any problem in their marriage was her fault, never his. When he became physically abusive to Rita, I told her she needed to call the police and get into counseling, but she wouldn't do either. She was truly afraid of Bill. Terribly afraid."

"Did you see any physical evidence of the physical violence on Rita's person?" asked Doug.

"She showed me her arms one time. She was wearing long sleeves to hide the bruises, but pulled her sleeves up so I could see. She said she was pretty battered all over."

"Did Rita ever confide to Amy or show her some of the injuries caused by Bill?"

"I don't know. You'd have to ask Amy. My ex-wife pretty much had her head in the sand most of the time. If it didn't involve our two kids, she wasn't interested in listening."

"So did Rita ever press charges or take Bill to court for domestic violence?"

"As I said, she was too scared."

According to Rita, she had taken Bill to court several times for domestic violence. Court records couldn't confirm that at all. Chaz realized from Rita's interview with him that it had already been checked.

"Did you speak to Bill about the physical abuse or confront him?"

"No, never. It wasn't my place."

"Did Bill know Rita was sharing their melees with you?"

"Of course not! She had to talk to someone or she'd go crazy."

"Usually women turn to their mothers or sisters or close female friends—perhaps someone like Amy rather than a male neighbor, so that seems highly unusual that she would have shared only with you."

"So what are you suggesting, Mr. Conrad?"

"Well, there was never any evidence of domestic violence toward Rita— except Rita's word—and yours, of course, and there was no evidence whatsoever that Bill was ever violent to Ivy. Usually men have a pattern with that. In fact, evidence from everyone who knew Bill and Ivy intimately and from Ivy's own private journals indicate Bill was indeed a 'gentle spirit' and a good husband."

"People change, Mr. Conrad. Even if all of this is true, what does that have to do with their murders?"

"Andy believed for all of these years that his dad was mean. Mean to his mom and that eventually destroyed the relationship between him and his father. Then if Andy believed he had been cheated out of money he had coming to him, he could become bitter. Andy seems to be struggling right now to make ends meet, and perhaps he became resentful his dad wasn't sharing some of his spoils to help him. So if this good-for-nothing

dad AND his wife were dead, Andy believed he would inherit most of his dad's wealth since he was his closest living relative. After all, Andy is getting married soon and that money could come in awfully handy as he and Wendy begin their new life together."

"That is preposterous! So you think Rita influenced Andy to kill Bill and Ivy? No way! No way!

"Bill was an asshole for sure—a rich one—and Ivy seemed like a perfect match for him! Bill didn't deserve living the good life. We're all glad those two are out of our lives forever, but none of us killed them. None of us!

"And as for Andy—he's not the sharpest kid in the world, and while it's true he's struggling financially, he would never kill his own dad for money. We haven't helped Andy financially because we want him to meet his own responsibilities and to learn to work hard for what he gets. Bill and Ivy were self-serving jerks! I personally blushed at their cheapness. They were callous and flippant toward Andy and hypocritical religious zealots!"

Chaz couldn't have been more defensive toward his family, and yet he couldn't have been more denigrating toward Bill and Ivy Chandler. Doug's theory had definitely struck a nerve. From Darrington's honest outburst, Doug seemed quite convinced that Chaz and Rita had nothing to do with the murders. Their household had been filled with lies and fabrications that had deeply influenced Andy. It had to have had an affect on a young child which would carry throughout his teen years. Doug could tell that Chaz totally believed in Andy's innocence. Could Doug be totally wrong about Andy's involvement or was Chaz naïve and blinded to the evil web Rita and he had weaved in their home?

CHAPTER 61

Andy Chandler went through his workout quickly. He was on edge. He had been nervous, to say the least, knowing that Mr. Conrad had been coming around asking all kinds of questions about his dad's murder. If he was as good as his reputation, the case could conceivably be solved despite there being no witnesses or evidence, although he couldn't see how.

His mom and Chaz had been questioned too. His mom had called him immediately after Mr. Conrad had left and told him about their conversation, but he sensed his mom was withholding something.

As soon as he stepped inside his apartment, he had a message waiting. He hit the button:

"Hi, sweetie. It's me. I have tomorrow evening off. Hopefully, we can get together. I've picked out five invitations with matching napkins and programs that I'm considering for our wedding, and I want you to help me choose one. I also want to get an engagement picture taken for our notice in The Suburbanite. Call me! Love ya!"

Just hearing Wendy's voice picked him up. She was the one person in his life who seemed to love him unconditionally. She had always accepted him for who he was. She had all the qualities he admired in a woman. He loved her optimism and the fact that she was so non-judgmental of others. That was priceless. When he was with Wendy, his heart truly raced.

He wasn't the least bit interested in sharing in the selection of wedding invitations—whatever she liked was fine by him— but he had learned early on in their engagement to fake excitement about all of the plans. Yes, he looked forward to their wedding day, but, really, he just wanted to marry Wendy and get on with their lives. He didn't deserve her. He had made some serious mistakes in his life already, but he committed himself to walking upright forevermore and making up for them.

He would be committed and loyal in his marriage to Wendy forever, and he wanted to have children and be a good father when that time came. He had done nothing but think about how wonderful his life would be with Wendy since the moment she had accepted his wedding proposal.

But the events of the past few days had cast a shadow on those dreams. It seemed like he was living a façade. His happiness had left him, and he felt as though he was getting swept out to sea. Could he let Wendy continue making plans for a wedding that might not take place?

Andy knew he had to confront his mother about his childhood. Everything in his future was pending on her answers. She had always been so open and candid with him. He always felt she tried to protect him from hurtful things his dad did as a non-custodial parent, but Mr. Conrad had come along and shown him evidence that refuted most of what his mother had told him about his dad. There had to be a valid explanation. He needed the answers soon because he was feeling his life starting to spin out of control.

He picked up the phone and dialed his mother's phone number. This would be the most important phone call of his life.

CHAPTER 62

D onna Gifford arrived at Classic Hair Salon a few minutes after Rita Darrington had arrived for her appointment. Both were called to their hairdresser's chair at the same time. Rita immediately recognized Donna and asked her how her divorced friend was doing.

"Well, she's not divorced yet. They're still in the paperwork process."

"Oh, that's right. I hope she's hired a devious lawyer. She shouldn't be looking for a fair settlement for the two of them. She should be seeking what's best for her, and that needs to happen right from the get-go.

"Hi, Kim. I need a cut and color job today. You know the routine. I'm looking for a new and exquisite hairstyle for our upcoming wedding."

"Gotcha. I think I have the perfect style in mind for you, Rita, so let's get to work!" said Kim.

"Hi, Carla."

"Hi, Donna. So how did you like the perm last week?"

"I loved it. It gave me just enough body so that my hair looked full and healthy. I just need a shampoo and set today."

"Sure thing. I see you and Rita are continuing the saga where you left off last week," Carla said with a chuckle.

"Well, it's always good to hear different ways of approaching a divorce, I guess. This is my friend's first experience with divorce. And *since she has a child, it is so much more challenging and important she do the right thing,"* said Donna.

Rita spoke up. *"Well, I've been divorced twice. With my first divorce to Rick Morgan I was much too young and naïve, but in my second divorce I could afford the best divorce lawyer in town who was notorious for fighting for women's rights. So let's just say I won on every count and my ex—husband lost on every one,"* Rita laughed.

"Tell your friend to move to the farthest end of the county and have the court require her ex to do all of the driving. With the cost of gas prices today and the time it takes him to get over to her house to pick up his son, he will want to miss many of his visits. Or, he can't get off work and get to his son's school events on time, so eventually he'll simply give up or will just go now and then to them."

"So was your son aware of what you were doing to discourage his father from seeing him?" Donna asked, making an effort to sound polite.

"Well, no, of course not! He was much too young. But when my son got older and he would rather go do something with our family during his midweek visitation, we either vacated our house early so that when my husband drove all the way across town and knocked on our door, no one was home. Sometimes we didn't get out of the house in time, so we turned off all of the lights and hid in the back room where he couldn't see us. He would call into the house and leave a message that he was waiting for Andy at the door. After about ten or fifteen minutes of waiting in the car for our return, he would leave. Then we'd go to the arcades or movies and have a great family outing. The next day I'd call Bill's house and leave a message, stating we were out shopping for supplies for a school project Andy had and totally lost track of the time. I'd apologize and then I'd tell Andy my story so he could confirm it with his dad. Andy was more than willing to go along as he loved playing the arcades or going to the movies. I knew Bill was upset, but there wasn't really anything he could do about it. After all, would he take me to court for an innocent mistake and for helping our son with a school assignment?"

"*So how old is your son now?*" Donna asked, knowing the answer before she asked it.

"*Andy is twenty-five years old.*"

"*So is he functioning in life okay? Didn't you say his dad was murdered?*"

"*Yes, along with his wife. But Andy is doing just fine. He has an okay job at Akron General Medical Center and is engaged to be married November 28th. I think down the road he will be inheriting a rather large sum of money from his father once the murders get solved.*"

"*Won't it be sad for Andy that his own dad won't be at the wedding?*"

"*I don't think so. Andy didn't care for my ex's new wife. Well, he did at first, but when she started setting rules in their house for Andy, we told him he didn't have to listen to her at all. He did have to mind his father because that was his parent and his Dad's house. But Bill wasn't gifted with parenting skills, so he left the discipline and the running of the house up to Ivy. Ivy wasn't related to Andy. In fact, we told him he didn't even have to speak to her when he spent the weekends over there if he didn't want to. And I think he chose not to. So, no, I really don't think he misses either of them.*"

"*Wouldn't it have been a happier life for your son if Andy could have felt comfortable and loved in both homes? You seemed to have interfered with his relationship with his dad so early on that he could have, otherwise, had the best of both worlds,*" said Donna sincerely.

Everyone in the salon got silent and looked at Rita to watch her response. No one had ever had the guts to challenge Rita's child rearing tactics when she bragged about doing those things to her ex-husband.

"*My son was loved by his new family. It was a blended family with Chaz's kids, but we were like the Partridge family. Andy has had a great life, and we were all he needed,*" Rita said defensively.

"*Didn't Andy feel cheap when he was hiding from his dad or when lying to him? What values were you instilling in him?*"

Every patron was listening to every word being spoken between Donna and Rita with rapt attention. They awaited Rita's answer with bated breath.

"I don't think he felt cheap. We taught him at a young age to be independent. Life is too short not to do what you want in life. He was such a quiet, passive child, and he was very respectful to those in authority—"

"Except toward his father and stepmother." Donna finished the line for Rita.

"Divorce is rough. Kids learn to adjust to those life changes or adapt in a way they find acceptable to them. Andy did that. He's a good boy and we're very proud of him." Rita was starting to feel uncomfortable and wanted to change the topic, but Donna continued on.

"Parental alienation syndrome is the active blocking of access or contact between a child and the absent parent. It can have serious consequences for a child. Maybe even a latent reaction during adulthood. I really don't think my friend wants to follow that path," said Donna in a very non-judgmental tone.

"Well, it worked just fine for us," Rita declared rather surly.

"I surely hope so." said Donna sweetly.

Both ladies began to talk to their own stylist. Donna could clearly see the family dynamics that went on in the Darrington home and how the relationship deteriorated between Andy and Bill and Ivy. The last conversation with Rita pretty much confirmed her suspicions about the psychological damage that was done to Andy. It was so troubling to her. She had a degree in behavioral science, and from the information she and her team had gathered, the serial killer theory could be shelved.

She needed to get back to the office to make a call to Dr. Brandon White, APD's criminal profiler to pick his brain. After that, she knew Doug would want to get the team together to pool their facts and confirm whether they were moving the investigation in the right direction. As much as she hoped they weren't, in her heart she knew they were.

CHAPTER 63

Donna returned to the office and put a call in to Dr. Brandon White. Fortunately, he was in his office and Donna explained who had hired them to work on the Chandler homicides. She gave him an update on what she had learned about Andy Chandler.

She described all of the many nice qualities about Andy—reports from his former teachers and principal, his school discipline record, and then the crazy family dynamics from age four until his high school graduation. She detailed for him some of the tactics used by Rita to alienate Andy from Bill and Ivy Chandler.

"So you can see, Andy had a pretty heavy load to carry as a kid. So what do you think, Dr. White?"

"Well, it isn't usually the load that weighs us down. It's the way we carry it," said Dr. White.

"His mother pulled quite a ruse on her son. I'm sure he formulated many undeserved, negative opinions about his father and stepmother over the years, but to him, they were real. All of us are where we are today—mentally, physically, spiritually, emotionally, and even financially because of how we think," he continued. *"Many of our sorrows can be traced to relationships with wrong people. Our infamous Quinton Reed was a perfect example of that."*

"He chose at age fifteen to *no longer honor his weekend and midweek visitations,"* explained Donna. *"He preferred being with his school friends and his residential parents. It seems by then he had turned*

his back on his father. Once the child support payments stopped, there was really nothing to connect them. Everything we've learned about the Chandlers confirmed they were good people and caring parents to Andy. They didn't deserve to be treated like that or to die that way."

"I certainly agree. This is a sad case, and I truly hope it gets solved. We are so low on manpower that our officers haven't had time to broaden their interviews as they should have or widen their investigation on this case. If it hadn't been Doug Conrad's company investigating this case, I know APD would never have shared those journals or autopsy reports with anyone, but we definitely need some help. We all hope to see this case wrapped up in the very near future."

"So do I. I so hope Andy Chandler's not our murderer, but everything seems to be pointing to him. He's a nice kid who's planning to get married at Thanksgiving time."

"Well, just remember, we all make choices and then our choices make us. Because of the way Andy was reared, he has a propensity toward self-serving behavior. He may have wasted valuable years imagining revenge upon his father for the heartache he falsely believed his dad had imposed upon his mother—and, indirectly, upon him.

"And if he's been a people pleaser for most of his life, then he struggled with cutting off his relationship with his father in order to keep his mother happy. One decision you make can change the world—or at least YOUR world. Do you think he has a guilty conscience that can be brought to the surface?" asked Dr. White.

"How do you mean?" asked Donna, seeking his input and thoughts.

"Well, God didn't always put in us the ability to make right decisions, but to make a decision, and then, if wrong, to make it right. Is Andy the kind of kid who would do that?"

"Hmmm. That's an interesting thought. I've never met Andy, but Doug and Barnabus have. I'll get their thoughts on that. If they think yes, then I think we can break him. Thanks for the perspectives and insights, Dr. White."

"You bet. Keep in touch, Donna, and say hello to Doug and Mitch for me. They were two of my favorites at APD. I miss 'em!"

CHAPTER 64

It was late in the evening and Andy was restless and feeling peculiarly nervous. He had been thinking about Doug Conrad's visit. He knew Conrad and another detective had met with his folks. He had initially been interviewed by the Akron police the day after his father and Ivy had been found slain in the basement. The officers wrote down his whereabouts the evening of the murders. He knew he had much of the evening covered but not during the crucial time period. His story, however, was viable and couldn't necessarily be disproved.

His life had been trouble-free up to this point, so there would be no reason for him to be a strong suspect. When questioned, he acted concerned about the murders but didn't overplay it. He explained the distant relationship he had over the years with his dad and his dad's wife. That was very feasible also.

He was asked about his father's will, and he admitted he didn't know if his dad even had one, but if he did, he didn't know who the beneficiaries were, nor did he care. That really was true except for the last part. He did care. He did figure that his dad would be giving him at least a sizable portion of his lucrative estate if not all of it. For the sake of the police investigation, he would never inquire about the will or look the least bit interested. Thus, eliminating perhaps a motive he might have for killing his father.

Andy figured if some chump didn't get arrested for the crime, and the case became cold, the authorities or prosecutors couldn't withhold the distributing of the will indefinitely. Eventually he would find out what was in the will and, hopefully, he would obtain a large sum of money. His dad might have even chosen to hand his only son the ownership of Chandler Corbox and the house. Whom else would he pass those things on to? If he could just remain patient, and he could, the answers would eventually be revealed, and he might enjoy the vast legacy with his new bride.

Well, things could go either very right or very wrong. The trepidation he was feeling at the present time revolved around his mother. She was strong-willed. He needed to talk to her but he feared a confrontation. He had to know the truth. He decided he was turning into a wreck and couldn't go another day without asking his mom about the information Doug Conrad had shown him.

It was 10:00 p.m. He picked up the phone and called his mom's house. Chaz picked up on the second ring.

"Hi, Andy. It's late. What gives?"

"I need to talk to Mom. Is she around?"

"I hope this isn't about the investigation. Your mom is starting to get edgy about all the questions. If you get her all upset, none of us will get to sleep tonight. So can this wait?" asked Chaz.

"No, it can't. I have something I need to talk to her about."

"I'll check with her. Hold on."

Sometimes Chaz got under his skin. Who is he that he should prevent me from talking to my mom if I want to? thought Andy. About a minute passed before he heard his mother pick up an extension.

"Hi, honey. What's up?"

"Mom, Doug Conrad came to my apartment yesterday and asked me a lot of questions."

"I think we've all been bombarded by him, Andy, or at least someone from his firm. I forget the guy's name that spoke to me. It's normal to question family in a murder case, honey."

"Well, I need to know some things . . . about dad. I need the truth."

"Okay, son. What's on your mind?"

"Did dad really abuse you physically?"

"Yes. I've told you that before, Andy, but I just don't like talking about it."

"Did he hurt you, Mom?

"Why, of course, he hurt me!"

"How serious were your injuries?"

"What's this all about, Andy?"

"Mom, I just need to know."

"He bruised me too many times to count, he sprained my arm and wrist once, and I had a laceration above my eyebrow once."

"Did you ever have to go to the hospital for medical treatment?"

"I probably should have but I didn't."

"Did you ever call the police and report it?"

There was a long pause and then a sigh.

"Yes, several times."

"What became of it?"

"Bill talked me into dropping the charges."

"So nothing ever went to court?"

"No," Rita answered almost inaudibly.

"Why didn't you decide to press charges and go after him, Mom?"

"I guess I was afraid. Maybe ashamed. As I've told you before, I simply decided to leave and get away from him. The entire marriage was a poignant experience. I had had one failed marriage, and I wasn't going to live through another bad one if I could help it."

"So did you tell Grandma and Grandpa about Dad hurting you?"

"No."

"Why not?"

"I didn't want them getting involved."

"Did they ever see your injuries?"

"No, I always hid them."

"You said Dad failed to pay his child support at times. Was that true?"

"Yes. Most definitely."

"How many times would you say he failed to pay?"

"I'm not sure. Quite a few. And many times he was late in paying it. What's this all about, Andy?"

"You told me you took Dad to court over his failure to pay, right?"

"Why, yes. I had to. I had no source of money coming in to support you. I had to go after him to make him pay."

"Then explain to me why there are no Summit County court records showing you ever took Dad to court for child support!"

"I don't know. It was a long time ago. Maybe they delete them after so many years. Or perhaps they store them away somewhere, and they get lost. I can't explain it. But why should I have to?"

"Mom, Mr. Conrad had proof of all of Dad's child support payments from the time I was four years old until I graduated from Ellet. He proved Dad paid on time and never missed a payment. He showed me the proof!"

"Well, in court it was determined the payments got lost in the mail or were delayed because of a computer glitch at the Child Support Bureau. The computers would shut down and then it would take several days to get them up and running before they could mail them out. I couldn't have known that."

"Mom, there were no court records you ever took Dad to court for not paying child support."

"That's just not true, Andy."

"Did Dad refuse to pay my medical bills?" Andy asked.

"He didn't at first, but after he married Ivy, he began to question all of your medical bills. He didn't believe they were real and so he refused to pay."

"Mom, the court record shows you never submitted the bill to the insurance company, so Dad didn't even know about the bill. By the time he found out about it, a year had passed and the insurance company refused to pay the claim. You claimed Dad was a deadbeat father and he was forced to pay 100% of that bill."

"It was an honest mistake on my part, but your dad was required to pay for all of your medical bills, no matter what!"

"Was it an honest mistake, Mom?"

"I don't like your tone nor your insinuation, Andy!" retorted Rita.

"So, now I have a question for you, son. Did you kill your father? Please tell me you didn't kill your father. Did you?"

Dead silence at the other end. Tears streamed down Rita's cheeks as she waited for his answer. Almost two minutes had passed before Andy replied.

"No, Mom. I didn't. It seems like we have a lot in common."

"What does that mean, Andy?"

She heard a click and then the disconnect.

"Andy? What does that mean? Answer me!" She screamed into the dead phone. Rita sat in the chair by her bed and wept bitterly. She was confused and afraid.

CHAPTER 65

The team meeting in the conference room at Conrad Confidential was productive. As each one shared information they had gleaned from their various interviews, the picture seemed clear that Andy had most likely acted alone in the homicides. There was still no actual proof that Andy was guilty of the Chandler murders. Zap had learned that Andy had some experience with smaller guns and that, by his own admission, he had to be near his target to actually hit it. The Chandlers had been shot at close range, execution-style. They needed to find the weapon, but so much time had passed, it would be like finding a needle in a haystack. But, the killer would know where it was.

The motive for the killings was most likely for the inheritance, but what Andy didn't know at the time of the murders, nor did he know now, was that he had been clearly written out of his father's will and would never be receiving so much as a dollar from the estate.

He killed his father on a false assumption, very likely prompted by his mother who led him to believe there would be a pot of gold at the end of the rainbow.

Mitch had pulled out some selected portions of Ivy's journal. This time, the team decided that Mitch and Doug, both great father figures, should pay a visit to Andy at his apartment. Andy told them he was meeting his fiancée, Wendy, at 6 p.m. for dinner, so he only had fifteen minutes to give to them. They agreed to meet at 5:25 p.m.

Doug introduced Andy to Mitch Neubauer, his partner. Andy thought it was cool to meet both men who were involved with the Conrad murder. He remembered that Mitch had been quite a hero and had sustained major injuries protecting the Conrad children. He admired both men, but he also feared them.

Mitch began.

"Andy, we are getting closer to solving this case, but we need to ask you some pretty serious questions. Do you own any guns?"

"No. I told the police that already."

"Whether you own one or not, are you or have you been in possession of any guns in the past year?"

"No."

"We have reason to believe you went target practicing within the year. Is that true?"

"Yes. So what? My father is a hunter, and he sets up a target shooting area in his backyard."

"Your dad?" asked Mitch.

"Well, my stepdad. Chaz Darrington."

"Do you always call him Dad?"

"Yes. My mom asked me to. He was the father figure in our home where I grew up, so it made sense."

"So have you shot guns in your stepdad's backyard in the past year?"

"Maybe once or twice."

"And what guns did you fire?"

"I think my dad had a .22 and a .38 special."

"You think or you know?"

"I know."

"Did you ever buy a gun from someone off the street or from someone you knew—a friend, acquaintance, or relative?"

"No," Andy responded with hesitation. *"And I didn't kill my father! I hadn't seen my dad for nearly ten years. But when I did visit him, we never, never argued about anything. I can never even remember him raising his voice at me or spanking me. So why—out*

of the clear blue—would I go over to his house and kill him and his wife?"

Doug decided to enter into the conversation at that point.

"Well, we'll come back to that in just a minute, but you bring up a good point. Your dad had the reputation for being a very kind and gentle man. I counted over 450 names on the guestbook at Bacher's Funeral Home of those who came to pay respect to your dad and Ivy. Many were employees and customers of your dad's. That in itself speaks to the character and integrity of your father. Lots of colleagues and students came to see Ivy too. Lots of tears were shed in those two days, and family members shared some of the comments with us from those people. Your parents were highly respected and loved. It tells a story, Andy. How does that saying go . . . 'When you were born, you cried and others rejoiced. Live your life in such a way so that when you die, you rejoice and others cry.' I think you were a luckier kid than you knew."

Andy's eyes filled up with tears and he kept shaking his head side to side.

Mitch responded, as they decided to turn up the heat on Andy.

"So let's talk about the motive. Your motive was as old as dirt. Money. Your dad was worth over a million dollars. Alive you weren't getting anything, but dead you had a chance, especially if Ivy were dead too. You would be your dad's closest living relative, and you figured surely you'd get a huge chunk of change."

"I still don't know if my dad even had a will."

"Doesn't matter. You'd get a settlement by being his closest relative."

"So did my dad have a will?" asked Andy.

Mitch and Doug knew they couldn't compromise the APD investigation, so Mitch responded, *"That information hasn't been released yet. You'd have to ask Sgt. Parker who's leading the homicide case about that."*

Doug chimed in. *"Your father and stepmother were both well educated. With their wealth it would be unusual for them not to have their estate protected should something happen to them."*

"Andy," Mitch said, *"We think your mom turned you against your father. It's called parental alienation syndrome. She wanted you to believe you only had one family—hers with Chaz Darrington. She tried to invalidate your father, and since you were so young, you were easily influenced. She had an insatiable need to have control over your father, and domestic court, unfortunately, tends to turn her head away from protecting the rights of fathers. Your mom manipulated your thinking during your impressionable years. She fabricated stories about your father to create favorable public impressions of her."*

"My mom would NEVER lie to me! Everything she ever did for me was in my best interest," shouted Andy as his emotions were building up.

"We know this is a very hurtful and unflattering depiction of your mother, Andy, and yet these are traits highly predictable in self-centered narcissists, who we believe your mother is," said Doug in the most gentle tone.

"Well, you're dead wrong about my mother, and you're wrong about me! I can't take this anymore. I want you to leave!" shouted Andy.

"We're sorry, Andy, but two good people are dead before their time. People who loved Bill and Ivy can't just let their murders go unsolved. They need closure and justice. It's best for everyone that justice gets served.

"If you did it, we will find the proof to convict. You'd be better off to come clean, but either way, our investigation is closing in, and we will find the killer. We truly hope you didn't do this. We think you are a fine young man who may have made a terrible mistake, and we're willing to help you, son, if you did do this. You need to calm down before you get behind the wheel of the car. We don't want anyone else getting hurt. Here's my business card if you ever need to talk. We wanted to share a few comments from Ivy's journal, but there isn't time. I think you would find it an eye-opener," said Doug. *"How about if we just leave these here and you can read them at your leisure?"*

"Fine," said Andy and he set them on his kitchen table.

Both men reached out and shook Andy's hand before leaving. It wasn't the normal way a police officer would leave a home with a possible murder suspect, but Andy wasn't your typical murderer. Doug and Mitch were fathers of sons. This was gut-wrenching for them. They hoped beyond hope that Andy was truly innocent. A nice kid with a pretty evil mother—it was so unjust.

CHAPTER 66

A ndy quickly walked to his Silverado truck in the parking lot and started it up. His head was swimming from the short ten minute meeting he had with Mr. Conrad and his partner. It was, in his mind, a clear confrontation. He had become the prime suspect, and yet if authorities had had any proof, he would have been arrested by now. It had been almost two months since the murders, and, apparently, no new evidence had appeared. If Grandma Porter and Aunt Alayna hadn't hired private detectives, Andy felt the murders would have gone unsolved as the A.P.D. were understaffed and had released over thirty police officers. There were many officers who were transferred to different departments and given different assignments, so it was quite a distraction.

He had so much to think about after this visit. The last thing he wanted to do now was pick out wedding invitations and discuss wedding plans. He just wanted to run away with Wendy. Now he wasn't even sure there was going to be a wedding. Was it even fair to Wendy to marry her with all of this going on?

He pulled in to Wendy's driveway and walked up to her apartment door. Just as he was about to knock, the door flew open and Jackie, Wendy's roommate, greeted him with a smile as she was on her way out. Fortunately, Jenny, Wendy's other roommate, was already gone for the evening, so they had the apartment all to themselves for a change.

Wendy had seen Andy pull in to the driveway from their kitchen window and rushed to the door to greet him with a big hug and kiss. She was the one person who could make all of his worries evaporate. She felt so good in his arms. Her hair smelled fragrant and her skin was so smooth and soft. He was so lucky to have her. He had not been very lucky with girls until Wendy came along. He just didn't have a way with them. He wasn't a very good conversationalist, for one thing, but neither was he an academic achiever or a sports jock. He really wasn't sure what Wendy actually found attractive in him.

"Hi, Sweetie! Good day? Come over to the kitchen table. I have all of the invitations and programs spread out for you to look at," she said all in one excited breath.

Andy's mom had given him some good advice and tips on handling this evening of decision making: *Find out what Wendy likes best and then agree with her. Look interested in it, but agree on everything she wants.*

Chaz had added his two cents' worth: *"Happy wife, happy life!"* so *keep your mouth shut and just go along with the program. No matter what you like, she'll end up choosing the one she likes anyway, so cut to the chase and agree. Since you don't care either way—it's a win win situation.* All three of them laughed.

He felt well coached, so when they walked over to the table, she presented him with five choices. He looked at each one carefully and said, *"They're all so nice. Which one do you like best?"*

She pointed to the one at the top left.

"That's the one I like the best, too," he said.

"Really? Really, Andy? You like it too? Honestly?"

"Yeah. I really do. I like it a lot, and the program to match it as well."

"Cool! We are so compatible. I'll order the thank you notes to match, and then I think we need to find favors and then most everything is done. I've got my dress. The bridesmaid dresses have been ordered. We've picked out the tuxedoes. We've chosen the florist and photographer, so

we just need to meet with the pastor for counseling. When do you want to do that?" she asked nonchalantly.

"Counseling? Why do we need that?"

"Well, first, the pastor won't agree to marry us without counseling, and, secondly, it's probably a good idea to talk about some serious issues before marriage to assure we get started with no surprises or get off on the wrong foot. So, yeah?" she said all bubbly.

"What kind of things will we be talking about?" asked Andy who was totally clueless about that. He had no idea that was a requirement.

"Oh, things like our love language, money management, child rearing, in-law problems, roles, religion, sex . . . things like that," she answered.

"So is it just one session?"

"No, I think it's four one hour sessions in the evening—whatever time works for us."

"Four one hour sessions? Are you kidding me?" Andy said, unable to hide his shock.

"He won't marry us if we don't do this, Andy. It's for our good. We have to do this."

"Okay. I'll look at my calendar, but it has to fit around my workouts at the Y."

"It'll be a good thing. You'll see!" she assured him.

"I just hope when we discuss all of these issues that you'll still want to marry me," said Andy earnestly.

"That's what you're worried about?" Wendy asked.

"No, not really, but it is a possibility. I mean . . . it is possible, isn't it?"

"I guess there's a remote chance. Why? Are you going to hit me with some surprises?"

"I might. Are you prepared?"

"It depends on what it is, I guess," said Wendy.

"We all have a past, Wendy. We've all made mistakes. Some are more serious than others. Life can be . . . well . . . complicated," said Andy with a serious look on his face.

"So what are you trying to say here, Andy?"

"A lot has happened to me recently—especially with the murders of my dad and Ivy. I love you, Wendy, and nothing will ever change that."

"And I love you, Andrew Chandler. I'm ready—well, almost ready—to become Mrs. Andrew Chandler!" Wendy said with a big, reassuring smile. *"So I had better get to purchasing these wedding invitations,"* she said.

"Wendy, can you wait until maybe the latter part of next week to do that?"

"Why?" she asked concerned and a bit curiously.

"There are some things going on in my life right now that need to be resolved. I'm not sure how things are going to end."

"What do you mean, Andy? What's going on in your life that needs to be resolved?"

"Just things," he repeated.

"You're scaring me, Andy. Does this have something to do with your father's death?" she asked sincerely.

"I'm confused by it all. So maybe that counseling will be a good thing, after all," he said optimistically.

Wendy smiled but she sensed something was wrong. She wanted to dig a little deeper and ask Andy more questions, but he seemed so troubled in spirit so she decided to save it for another day. Something was definitely festering inside the man she loved, and she was going to have to get to the bottom of it by next week.

CHAPTER 67

Andy was home and in the bed by midnight. He was emotionally distraught and on the brink of hyperventilating. His world was falling apart and he knew it. He really couldn't blame anyone but himself. He found it despicable when criminals would blame their parents or school or genetics or circumstances of everyday life for their mistakes. It was always someone else's fault. The ultimate outcome of anyone's life is a matter of personal choice. If it's true that our thinking creates a pathway to success or failure, as Mr. Maxwell his principal told him on the day he was about to suspend him for fighting, then he had somehow stepped off an acceptable path and on to one that would now lead him to utter failure and self-destruction. He was persistent toward a goal that became insanity, and he couldn't explain it to himself much less to anyone else.

He no longer recognized the person he saw in the mirror. He was never a person who would stand out in a crowd. He would always be just an *average* guy. But he never thought he would be pursued by the law.

Andy remembered the journal that Mr. Conrad and Mr. Neubauer had left for him to read. He had set it on the card table in the kitchen and had temporarily forgotten about it.

He quickly got out of bed and went into the kitchen to retrieve it. He returned to bed and turned his three way lamp to the highest voltage and began to scan the journal. Someone had randomly taken pages out of Ivy's journals over the years, so nothing was in consecutive order, not that it really mattered. Andy began to read the excerpts in Ivy's own handwriting:

Andy said he couldn't wait until Bill and I married so we could all be one happy family. That's what I want too. I'm very excited about being a stepmother. Andy is so sweet.

The neighbor boys made fun of Andy today. He came inside the house sobbing. I marched over to their house and spoke to their father. It should never happen again. Bill and I try so hard to protect Andy's tender and sensitive heart.

Bill drove over to Ellet to pick Andy up for our midweek visitation. I stayed home to make Andy's favorite meal. Bill came into the house with no Andy. No one was home. Bill felt they were in there, but no one would come to the door or answer the phone. Both of us had looked forward to his visit. The Darringtons are cruel.

Andy came in the house and ran straight up to his room. Bill and I always have some sort of new toy or gadget on his bed waiting for him when he comes for the weekend. Andy loves gadgets.

I worked all evening putting our July vacation pictures on a corkboard that's on Andy's bedroom wall. It should remind him of all the fun we had in Yosemite National Park. What great fun we had whitewater rafting on Merced River, horseback riding in Yosemite Valley and hiking to Bridalveil Fall.

Andy spent the weekend with us but he hardly spoke to us. We tried to engage him in conversation—about school, his friends, but he was tight lipped. I noticed he never said hello back to me when he walked into the house. We have waited two weeks to see him and share time together, but he's so unresponsive. I don't think it's simply teenage behavior. It seems quite deliberate and staged. We don't deserve to be snubbed.

Andy cancelled coming to our house for the third time in the past two months. We haven't seen him for weeks. We call over to the Darrington home. We're told Andy isn't home. We leave a message for him to call us. He never does. We're not positive he's even been given the message. He's breaking our heart. I can only imagine how hurt Bill is. This is his only child.

We drove across town to see Andy perform in a school play. He did a great job! We couldn't wait to tell him so either. We know Andy saw us sitting in the audience, but afterward, he never came out to talk to us. We went home feeling unappreciated and dejected.

We love Andy so much, but we know we're losing him. We've invested so much of our time in him, but we get nothing back from him. We tell him all the time how much we love him. He never responds back or even acknowledges our feelings.

Andy called Bill on Father's Day and told him he had decided not to stay over anymore for weekend visitations or visit midweek. It was Father's Day, for God's sake! Bill was crushed. If only Andy knew how much we love him and long to have him in our lives . . . why would he hurt his dad like that? Why? He obviously chose that particular day to inflict upon his father the deepest hurt possible.

We went to Andy's high school graduation even though we weren't invited. I tried to take a picture of him as he walked by us before ascending the stage to receive his diploma. He turned away so I could only get his backside. How mean is that? Where is this mean behavior coming from? What did we do to deserve this kind of treatment? We really don't know.

We have asked Andy on numerous occasions to tell us what is bugging him about us. We want to be a united and happy family again. He refuses to talk to us or tell us what the issues are.

For years I collected Andy's school pictures. I put them in a big oval picture frame with every year of his life and planned to give it to him at graduation, but he refused to give us his last three years' pictures, so I couldn't complete the project and present the gift to him. It is mind boggling to us. We have so much love to give to him. Who in his right mind rejects genuine love?

Tears were streaming down Andy's cheeks. Everything she wrote was true. Reading her thoughts, he could feel the love that his dad and Ivy had for him.

Andy's mother and stepfather were never religious, even though they attended a church now and then. Chaz had always bragged about some of the unethical things he did in his business that brought him a heftier paycheck or how he tricked Uncle Sam on his tax filings. His mother always threw her power around to get him out of some minor scrapes at school. So, of course, he processed all of that as *everybody does stuff like this and gets away with it.* He had heard his mother deliberately lie to lots of people. She always justified it, making wrong sound right, and she usually got her way.

But things weren't working out for him. He thought he was going to get away with something, but he didn't realize that eventually you do *reap what you sow.* He was up against a giant, and there was no way he could win.

He had thrown everything good away—and all over one day in his life. He wasn't sure what tomorrow would bring. Funny how as a kid he was afraid of the dark, but now as an adult, he was afraid of the light.

Andy had wanted to stay all night with Wendy tonight, but he didn't want her pressing him for answers to what was really bothering him. He wasn't ready to face the truth or the consequence, and he didn't want to act depressed around her. Instead, they drove to a park and took a long, brisk walk. They held hands and talked a lot about their upcoming wedding and some of the out of town relatives who were planning on attending. As Wendy said, *"It's going to be one great party!"*

Just before he left her apartment to go home, he put his arms around her and held her close to him. He couldn't let go. She could feel his warm breath on her neck and felt him kiss her cheek tenderly. She heard him sniffle and pushed back in time to see a few tears trickle down his cheeks.

"Andy. What is wrong? Please tell me. You're scaring me!"

"Nothing, Wendy. I'm just overwhelmed by you. I've never loved anyone like I've loved you. You are the best thing that has ever happened to me."

He cupped his hands around her face and kissed her ever so gently and sweetly before turning to leave. It was a kiss she'd never forget.

Andrew Chandler swept her off her feet. She didn't need an Einstein or a sports jock. Nope. All she needed was Andrew Chandler.

———

CHAPTER 68

At 1:00 a.m. Wendy called Andy. The phone rang and rang, but Andy didn't pick up. She knew he had to be home. Perhaps he was in a deep sleep and didn't hear the phone, OR he could be ignoring her call. He had caller ID. He knew when he left her apartment that she was worried about him.

She hung up and sat in a chair for awhile thinking about what she should do. She tried calling him a second time, except this time she let it ring six times—long enough for Andy's recorded greeting on his answering machine to come on.

"*Andy, it's me. If you're awake, pick up. I'm worried about you . . . we need to talk . . . pick up, honey . . .*"

Andy listened with agony, but he refused to pick up. He couldn't talk to Wendy about what was going on, especially not over the phone. She did deserve an explanation, however.

Wendy hung up and just as he suspected, she called again. She was persistent. She waited for the answering machine to pick up again.

"*Andy, please. I'm so worried about you. I know something is terribly wrong. I can tell you are overwhelmed right now about something. What is it? Are you having an emotional meltdown about your dad? Has his death finally hit you? Whatever it is, we'll get through it together, baby. Just pick up. Let's talk,*" she insisted with desperation.

Andy started to cry. He hadn't cried for years. Oh, he had cried on the inside plenty of times, but never on the outside. He was emotional, for sure. Everything he had believed about his father may not have been true at all. The person he most believed in had deceived him, and now he didn't know who to trust.

He could hear Wendy crying and his heart was breaking. He picked up.

"Wendy . . ."

"Andy, I'm here . . ."

"Wendy . . ." Andy tried to choke back the tears so he could talk but words wouldn't come.

"Are you okay, honey?" Wendy asked.

"No, not really."

"Is it your dad? Is the murder finally sinking in?" she asked as sensitively as she knew how.

"Yes. Yes. That's it. My dad is dead. I was so mean to my dad—and Ivy too. My mother lied to me about my father. I wanted to believe my mother, but those detectives have shown me proof my mom lied."

Andy was crying so hard she could hardly understand him.

"Did you ask her about it?"

"Yes, yes. Several times. She keeps sticking to her story. I want to still believe her, but the proof just seems to be too strong. She duped me all of these years. Why would she do that?"

"Please, Andy. Don't cry. I'm coming over to see you. I'll be there in 15, 20 minutes!"

"No, I'm fine..It's too late. Don't come, Wendy. I'm serious! DON'T come!"

She hung the phone up and Andy went nuts. Wendy didn't understand. He didn't want her here. He needed time to process what he should do. He needed to be alone.

Wendy grabbed her cell phone and rushed out the door. She knew it was late, but she had to call Rita Darrington. She felt the situation warranted it. Rita seemed to be at least part of the problem, and Wendy felt perhaps Rita could be part of the solution. Andy needed to be calmed down, and Rita knew Andy better than anyone.

The phone began to ring at the Darrington residence.

"Hello?"

Thank, God. Rita had picked up.

CHAPTER 69

Rita threw on some jeans and a sweater, grabbed her jacket, and jumped into the Land Cruiser. It would take her at least twenty-five minutes to get to Andy's. She would call him on her cell phone.

He picked up on the second ring.

"Hi, Mom."

"Andy, what's going on? Talk to me."

"Actually, I think you are the one that needs to talk to me. I want the truth this time, Mom. You owe it to me, and then I'm going to share a truth with you. Fair enough?"

Rita listened but didn't reply to his comments.

"I'll be there in about twenty minutes, Andy. Just relax. Wendy's coming too."

"No, Mom. I don't want Wendy here. This is just between the two of us. Call Wendy and tell her not to come."

"Okay."

Rita called Wendy on her cell and found out Wendy was already on her way to Andy's.

"Wendy, he doesn't want you to come. I'm not sure why. He just wants to talk to me. I'll calm him down and talk to you tomorrow, okay?"

"Okay, Mrs. Darrington, but I think he's having a meltdown about the murders."

"I'm sure it's been hard on him. These damn detectives have been questioning him—actually all of us—and I think it has shaken him up. I think they gave him the impression he is a suspect in their murders. Can you believe that? Our sweet Andy? He'll be okay, Wendy. Go home and get some sleep. I'm sure Andy will call you in the morning and discuss all of this with you. I promise I'll call you too and fill you in. Got to go. I'm almost at his apartment."

When she hung up from talking to Wendy, she started thinking about Andy's words over the phone. He was demanding the truth from her. She didn't know how she was going to get around that. He would once again ask about Bill's violence and refusal to pay child support. She had given it a spin the other day when he confronted her, but apparently he wasn't accepting that story. What truth did he have for her? Whatever it was, she knew this wasn't going to be a pleasant conversation with Andy, but it sounded like he was in distress and in need of her help. What loving mother wouldn't go to her son during a crisis? Andy was twenty-five years old and about to be married. He had a great future ahead of him. He . . . we . . . would get through this minor ordeal. Mama will make it all better. She always does.

CHAPTER 70

W endy was over a third of the way to Andy's apartment when Mrs. Darrington called her and told her to go back home. She didn't plan on interfering if Andy only wanted to speak to his mother, but some small voice inside her insisted she continue to drive to Andy's apartment. She would stay in the shadows. Neither of them would know she was there.

Perhaps she could stand on the outside and overhear something. She was so curious as to what was going on. That lady at Macy's was right on. Maybe Andy did have some deep-seated issues with his parents from long ago and was having some latent symptoms show up now. Having parents who were murdered would have an affect on anyone. Andy seemed unmoved by it, she thought, but apparently he's been in denial these past two months and it's all coming to the surface.

Whatever this was about, his mom was involved. She had lied to Andy about his dad—what about, she didn't know—and Andy had proof she lied. So tonight he was demanding a moment of truth from her. Andy's mental state depended on it. She hoped Mrs. Darrington would be honest and this issue could be laid to rest for him once and for all.

According to Mrs. Darrington, the detectives thought Andy was a suspect in the murder of his parents. That is absurd! Andy would never do such a thing. He couldn't do such a thing, and he had no reason to do such a thing or she would know.

As she thought back on tonight's conversation with Andy, she did recall Andy talking about how *we all have a past* and *how we've all made mistakes . . . some more serious than others* and *how complicated life is*. Was he trying to tell her something then and he just couldn't? He was being rather evasive, and now she realized she wasn't seeing the picture he may have been trying to draw for her.

So why did he want her to wait until later next week to order their wedding invitations? He said he *wasn't sure how things were going to end*. What did he mean by that?

This was all so ominous. She was starting to connect some dots, and she knew she had to get to that apartment and see what was going on.

CHAPTER 71

Rita arrived at the apartment and went straight to the end apartment where Andy resided. She could see lights on through his thin curtains. Only one other apartment in the entire complex had lights on. Rita knocked on Andy's door, and he opened it immediately. He was wearing blue jeans, an undershirt, and a pair of sandals. She noticed that his eyes and nose were red from crying. She couldn't recall the last time Andy even showed emotion, much less cried. This was so out of character for him and incongruous that it left her a bit befuddled.

She hugged Andy and he hugged her back.

"*So what's this all about, Andy? What's upsetting you? If it's these detectives, you have to realize they're just doing their job. It will pass. As soon as they catch the killer, you can relax and, hopefully, find out if your frugal father passed down his riches to his only heir. In which case you will be rich and on Easy Street for probably the rest of your life. Who knew cardboard boxes could be so lucrative?*"

Andy told his mom to sit on the couch and Andy sat in the chair. His mother was studying his countenance.

"*So what's on your mind, son?*"

"*I want you to tell me about my dad when the three of us lived together.*"

"*What do you want to know specifically?*"

"*Well, first, I want only the truth, but—*"

"*Andy, I resent that statement. I have always been truthful with you.*"

"No, Mom, you haven't, but tonight you're going to be."

"I don't like your tone, Andy. I drove clear across town in the middle of the night because you were upset. I won't have you treat me disrespectfully. Do you understand me?"

She saw him reach under the cushion of his chair and pull out a small revolver. She froze with fear because he was pointing it directly at her.

"Andy, where did you get that? You're scaring me. Never aim a gun at anyone! Put it away! What in the world are you thinking?" she asked almost too scared to catch her breath. She felt confident this was just a scare tactic. Andy would never dream of using this on her. She was his mother, after all.

"This is not a joke, and you had better not try to play head games with me. Now answer my question. Describe the kind of man Dad was when we lived together as a family."

"Quit aiming that gun at me, and I'll tell you."

Andy laid the gun across his legs and was transfixed on his mother just as she was on him.

"We were young and your dad was working hard at making his business not only survive but thrive. He was a very smart businessman and was selective in choosing employees to help him build the business. He put long hours in and before long, he was making excellent money. We could tell he struck gold in the box business."

"Keep going," Andy ordered.

"Well, he traveled quite a bit and wasn't home several days out of the week. Life was lonely for me. Your dad would come home stressed, and start an argument that oftentimes escalated into violence."

"Lie! That's a lie!" shouted Andy, and he picked up the gun and aimed it right at Rita. He also cocked the gun.

"I want the truth, Mom. There was never any proof of that, so try again and get it right this time! You only get one more chance at this."

Rita didn't know if Andy was capable of shooting her or not, but he seemed to know she was lying. She couldn't take a chance of him shooting her, so she decided to tell him the truth. She could do damage control and restore her relationship with Andy another day.

"Okay, Andy. The truth. Your dad was a very nice man. He was a kind, compassionate man. Everyone loved your dad. He was respectful, polite, and industrious. He was also frugal. He was a money saver and investor of it, I felt, to a fault. He would get mad at me if I wanted to buy expensive things, but eventually I got them anyway."

"Did Dad ever lay hands on you to hurt you. Ever?"

The gun was still aimed at her head.

"Did he, Mom?"

Rita hesitated for a long time. She didn't want to answer the question, for she had fabricated stories for years about Bill's domestic violence in their home. She embellished the stories with every telling of it. She had slandered Bill's reputation throughout two communities and never thought twice about it.

"No," she confessed almost inaudibly.

"Say it again!" Andy demanded.

"No, he never touched me once," Rita confessed with tears streaming down her face.

"So why did you say he did and denigrate his reputation like that?"

"I don't know," Rita cried.

"Yes, you do. Why?" He held the gun steady.

"I wanted a divorce, and I could rouse more public sympathy from family and friends and be the one held up in high esteem, not Bill."

*   *   *

Wendy arrived at Andy's apartment and quietly stood outside the kitchen window. The thin curtains weren't completely closed, and she could see through the narrow opening. Andy had a gun pointed directly at Rita. She was crying, and he was asking her questions. She could hear almost the entire conversation through the window. This was such a serious situation that Wendy knew police intervention was needed. She raced to her car and called 911. She explained who the parties were that were involved in the verbal altercation, their location, who she was. She also explained that Andy Chandler was the one whose parents had recently been murdered. That got the officer's attention. Wendy explained that Andy was under duress and she thought he was harmless, but the family needed help.

The dispatcher instructed Wendy to return to her car, lock it, and wait for the police to arrive. The dispatcher then called Sgt. Parker at his home and made him aware of the situation. Sgt. Parker immediately got up and ordered police sent to Andy's apartment but only to assess the situation. He would be there in ten minutes. The police weren't to do anything unless they sensed Mrs. Darrington was in dire danger. Perhaps they could negotiate and get the hostage out safely and then talk Andy down. This could be the break in the Chandler case they needed.

The police arrived in minutes and spoke with Wendy who pointed to Andy's apartment. They told her to keep her car doors locked and not get out of the car for any reason.

The police quietly went to the kitchen window and peeked through the crack of the curtains. They saw Andy and Rita talking. Rita was crying and the gun was aimed at her. Their instructions were to wait for Sgt. Parker, so they continued to evaluate the situation.

"So did Dad ever default on paying child support for me or complain about having to pay?" Andy inquired.

"No, he didn't."

"Did he complain about the amount he had to pay?"

"No, he didn't."

"So all of this time, you lied about all of that. You never had to take him to court for any of that."

Rita shook her head no and continued to cry.

"Did Dad ever refuse to pay my medical bills or complain about having to pay for those?"

Rita kept shaking her head.

"I want to hear an audible answer," he ordered.

"No, no, he was very loyal and reliable about paying for any of your needed expenses."

"So why did you pose as a victim and accuse Dad of so many horrible things that he didn't do?"

"I wanted your dad out of our lives. He was an inconvenience. We had a new family, now, of which he wasn't a part. We didn't need him anymore, except he wouldn't go away."

"Go on," said Andy.

"My only other recourse was to get you to dislike your dad so that you would want to write him off, and maybe Bill would get discouraged and stop trying to obtain more time with you.

"But then Ivy came along, so there was someone who could be in the house with you if Bill was at work or traveling, so he could then easily maintain his visitation times.

"You seemed to like Ivy. I guess I was a little jealous of Ivy."

"A little jealous?" Andy interrupted.

"She had a college education and had a successful teaching career and seemed like a caring, creative stepmother. I didn't want her stealing your heart away from me, so I painted a nasty picture of her too."

The phone rang unexpectedly. They both jumped. Andy waited for the answering machine to come on. Both listened.

"Andy Chandler? This is Sgt. Parker. I and two other armed officers are right outside your apartment. We know you're armed and have your mother inside. We want you to put the gun down and you and your mother come out peaceably."

Rita felt a sense of relief. Andy was shocked. How did the police know?

"Did you call the police before you came, Mom?"

"No. I don't know how they knew. I swear, Andy. Please, though, do as they say. No one has to get hurt. We'll get through this together, Andy. You know I won't press charges."

"It's too late. I can't do that."

"Yes, yes you can, Andy. Yes, you can," Rita insisted.

Sgt. Parker waited.

"Andy, we're going to wait five minutes and if you don't come out, we're going to come in." He clicked off.

Wendy disobeyed the police and walked right up to the police stationed outside Andy's apartment.

"Please let me talk to Andy. I'm his fiancée. Maybe he'll listen to me. Please don't hurt him. He is harmless. Truly he is."

Sgt. Parker didn't agree with Wendy. His experience told him that Andy was much more dangerous than this young, naïve girl knew. However, if she could defuse the volatile situation so that no one got hurt, it was worth a try.

"Okay. Call in. He's not answering the phone, so leave a message. Maybe he'll pick up."

Wendy called in to the apartment and the recorded message came on. She then began to speak:

"Andy, it's me, Wendy. I love you and don't want anyone to get hurt. Please come out peacefully. I'm right outside your apartment. Please."

Andy walked over to the phone and picked up.

"Wendy, you shouldn't have come here. You don't understand. My whole life I've been duped by my mother. I'm finally extracting the truth from her about my dad. I need the truth—"

"Yes, but Andy—you need to put the gun down. Someone could get hurt. The police are going to break down your door in a few minutes if you don't cooperate. Let your mother go and come out."

"Wendy, I love you, but we won't be getting married. I've messed up your life too."

"Andy, don't say that! We are getting married. November 28th! We are!"

"Pass the phone over to Sgt. Parker." Wendy obeyed him.

"He wants to talk to you." She handed the cell phone back to Sgt. Parker.

"Okay, Andy. This is Sgt. Parker. What have you decided?"

"The only way this is going to end peacefully is if Mr. Conrad comes here. I need to talk to him. He's the only person I trust right now."

Sgt. Parker paused for a moment and, then he replied, *"You mean Doug Conrad, the detective?"*

"Yes," responded Andy.

"Okay, I'll see if I can get hold of him, Andy. Meanwhile, promise me you won't hurt your mom or yourself."

"Just get him here. I will let him into the apartment."

"Okay, but it's going to take time."

Sgt. Parker got Doug Conrad's home phone number and called him. It was 2:00 a.m. The phone rang and Doug was awakened from a deep sleep. A phone call at this hour only meant one thing: trouble. Doug's first thought was that something had happened to Paul or Taylor. His heart skipped a beat until he saw his caller ID identify Sgt. Parker.

"Hi, Dennis. What's up?"

"Doug, we have a hostage situation at Andy Chandler's apartment."

"Who's the hostage?"

"Andy's mother. He has her at gunpoint. We have the apartment surrounded by police and have vacated the neighbors living close by. We're trying to negotiate him out of there, but he's demanding you come. He wants you to go into the apartment and talk to him. He says you're the only one he can trust."

"I'll be there in fifteen minutes. Let him know that."

"And, Doug, we'll have a bullet proof vest ready for you."

"I have my own here, Dennis. I'll put it on. Whatever you do, don't force the issue with Andy. I'm pretty sure I can get the situation under control. He's not a violent kid. He's confused, but I'm pretty sure he killed the Chandlers, so don't underestimate the situation either."

Doug made a quick call to Mitch who, in turn, called Barnabus and Donna.

CHAPTER 72

S gt. Parker called back into the house, informing Andy that Doug Conrad was on his way and should arrive in about fifteen minutes.

"*Stay cool, man.*"

Andy and Rita heard the message but remained transfixed on each other.

"*I read pieces of Ivy's journal and what she wrote about me over the years. I hurt both of them so badly, but they still loved me unconditionally,*" Andy informed Rita.

"*And what pieces didn't they show you, Andy? So why don't you find out if they really loved you enough to keep you in the will. Huh?*" Rita suggested rather defiantly.

"*It doesn't make any difference now anyway, Mom. I really don't deserve it, but I'll never see a dime of it if they did.*"

"*And why is that, Andy? You are his only heir, and you'd be entitled to at least something.*"

"*Because I killed them, Mom. That's why.*" Andy confessed.

"*Andy, you didn't do this. Say you didn't! You couldn't have!*" Tears began to flow incessantly down Rita's cheeks. She began to sob and shake her head back and forth.

"*You're lying, Andy. I know you. You could never do such a thing. Deny it! Take it back!*" Rita cried out.

"That's my truth, Mom. This very gun took them both out."

"Why, Andy? Why?" asked Rita through her sobs.

"Because Dad hurt you physically. You had to divorce him to get away from the danger. Right?

"So you tore me away from my father and my home based on lies. And then you made me turn my back on dad. You made me believe he never wanted to meet his parental duties by supporting me or paying for my health bills.

"You convinced me that Ivy was coercing Dad into defying or challenging the shared parenting agreement and causing you problems—even to the point of costing you hefty legal bills.

"But none of that was true, was it? Was it? Not a shred of it! There are no court records to support your allegations, so you lied to me, didn't you?"

Rita nodded yes and continued to sob.

"So then I got out of high school and didn't have any money to go to college or buy a car. And now I have a low paying job with no potential for advancement, and my father was over at his house sitting in the bathtub with Ivy counting his millions, as you used to say. That's the picture you painted for me.

"So what happened to all that extra money, Mom, that wasn't spent on me? Did you save a portion of the child support for me or spend it on yourself? I've been thinking about that.

"You know I killed Dad and his money hungry wife so that I could get the money I thought he cheated me out of for all those years. The ironic thing about it is, I killed the wrong parent. I decided to pay Dad back for all the beatings he gave you too. I thought in my own sick perspective that night—justice was being served.

"I certainly didn't want to live in this crappy apartment my entire life, but I didn't have a good education to help me crawl out of the dark hole I dug for myself. And you—"

The phone rang and both sat there waiting for the message to come on.

"Andy. This is Doug Conrad. I'm right outside your apartment. I'm unarmed, but I would like you to release your mother, and then I'll come in and we can talk."

Andy rushed over to the phone and picked up.

"No, Mr. Conrad. I want you to join us. I want you to hear something."

"Okay. Will you meet me at the door?"

"No. I'm going to unlock the door. Count to ten and then come in."

Doug had been updated about the situation. The tenants above and beside Andy had been quietly vacated for their personal safety. Doug looked at Sgt. Parker while counting to ten.

"We'll cover your back the best we can, Doug. Are you sure you want to go in?"

"Yes, I'm sure." Doug then turned the doorknob and stepped into the apartment.

"Have a seat in the chair there," Andy instructed him.

Andy had pulled a card table chair into the living room so that their seating arrangement was like a triangle. All three were facing each other. Doug obeyed him. Andy was holding a .380 bodyguard Smith and Wesson. The same gun that had killed Andy's parents. If the gun was tested and matched forensics, it would be enough proof to arrest Andy for their murders. The case would be solved. Having seen the gun, Doug now sensed the gravity of the situation.

"So what has brought us to this place, Andy?" Doug asked calmly.

"Truth versus lies, Mr. Conrad. My mom has finally confessed that she lied to me for years about my dad. I believed my mom, but she lied about almost every aspect pertaining to Dad. I was duped. I couldn't forgive my dad for hurting my mother and cheating me out of child support money and every other bad thing my mother lied about."

Doug looked over at Rita and watched her continue to sob and wipe her tears. She kept looking down at her hands.

"So the untruths you were led to believe about your father festered in your heart, and you couldn't forgive him?"

"No, I couldn't."

"And so—" Doug deliberately left the sentence unfinished.

"And so, as I know you already know—I killed my dad and Ivy. I was getting married and needed the money—my entitled inheritance, or so I

thought. I have been living from paycheck to paycheck since I graduated from high school. I couldn't seem to crawl out of this deep, dark hole, and yet Dad and Ivy were wallowing in money. It didn't seem fair. Dad was a jerk.

"Now I realize just how mean I treated them. I thought at the time they deserved it, but after I read Ivy's journal, I realized that I had never once witnessed my father ever being angry in the house. He never yelled at Ivy. He was never moody or argumentative as my mother had described him. I also realized how hard Ivy worked on our relationship. I treated her like a non-entity. Isn't that what you told me to do, Mom? So I felt justified in mistreating Ivy Connivy. All I could think of was to please you, Mom.

"So you see, I killed two innocent people who actually loved me, and I killed them based on a lifetime of fallacies.

"I don't blame you entirely, Mom. I had a brain. I had eyes and ears. But I made the ultimate decision to do it, based on what I believed. I've been torn up inside ever since. I spied on them for weeks, studying their routines, and then one night Dad accidentally left the garage door up. They were out on the deck in the hot tub, so I came through the door leading in the house from the garage and snuck downstairs. I was wearing latex gloves and surgeon shoes from the hospital. I hit the circuit breaker so all of the house lights would go off.

"When Dad came down the basement with only a flashlight and was standing at the circuit breaker, I stepped out from behind the furnace. He saw my face just as I shot him. He knew it was me. And then when Ivy came down to check on Dad, she heard me before she saw me, but it was too late. So both knew it was me before they took their final breath."

Tears were streaming down Andy's face as he told the story. Doug had a hidden recorder on him, so he was getting all of this on tape.

"You should have seen the shocked looks on their faces when they saw me. I haven't been able to get it out of my mind since that night."

Before Andy lost control of his emotions, Doug needed to intervene.

"Andy, you were misguided by your mother. She never fathomed the harm she was doing to you, but you need to cleanse your soul of these crimes, and you need to forgive your mother."

"Yes, yes, Andy. Please, please forgive me. I was selfish and self-centered. I didn't mean to hurt you so deeply. I didn't realize how I was affecting you. You never communicated that to me. It's my fault! This is all my fault," Rita said as she wept.

"Forgiveness costs nothing, Andy, but it's worth millions. Forgiveness is something under your control. Forgive your mom and let her go," Doug suggested in a soft and tender tone.

"Yes, Andy. I beg you for forgiveness. We'll get through this. I will take the blame for everything. The courts, I'm sure, will show mercy to you when they hear our story."

"You need to leave now, Mom. Go."

Doug felt a relief at Andy's willingness to now release his mother, but he was still feeling anxiety. He sensed something ominous.

"Andy, walk out with me. Put the gun down," Rita begged.

"Sorry, Mom."

Before she got to the door, Andy got up from his chair and enfolded his arms around his mother.

"I love you, Mom, and yes, I forgive you. It was all my choice."

He kissed his mother on the cheek and turned her body toward the door. "Now go."

Rita turned to Doug with a look of desperation.

"Take care of my son. Get him out of here alive. Please." Rita walked out the door with tears streaming down her face and never looked back.

A policeman put his hand around her arm and quickly escorted her to the parking lot and into the back of his squad car for her personal safety. He told her he would be back soon, and he returned to join the others waiting outside Andy's apartment.

Sgt. Parker was relieved that the hostage got out alive, but he was still concerned about Doug's safety. Knowing Doug and his fatherly attributes, he could probably talk Andy into walking out peaceably. They decided to give Andy and Doug more time.

CHAPTER 73

Doug asked Andy if he could move over to the couch so that he could be more comfortable and they might converse a little easier.

"*That's fine, but don't make any attempt to disarm me.*"

"*That's a deal, Andy.*"

"*So, Mr. Conrad, I blame myself for all of this. As I got older, I guess I didn't take the time to analyze what I knew. I let my mom manipulate me and do all of the thinking for me. I didn't judge my dad or Ivy on the things I witnessed at their house but what my mother told me. I didn't see them as lies.*"

"*So now what, Andy? What's the plan?*"

"*I have no future. I've thrown away my opportunity to marry Wendy Graves, the love of my life. I've ruined her life too—at least for now. There is no hope for me at all.*"

"*I disagree, Andy. You had a lot of wonderful gifts to offer society. The tragedy of life is not that man loses, but that he almost won. But for one night in your life—and one mistake— you would have made it. You are the victim of brainwashing and parental alienation syndrome. It will be proven in court. You will have to serve time, but I, too, think you will be given a lighter sentence and will have time in your life to enjoy some freedom.*"

"*God won't be on my side, Mr. Conrad. I've murdered two people in cold blood and one is my own flesh and blood— my father. How low is that?*"

"It's not as important that God is on your side, Andy, as it is YOU are on HIS side. You can still have a useful life in prison."

"You're the only person in my life who talked to me straight and has been honest with me. You are a nice man, Mr. Conrad."

"Thanks for the compliment, son. How about if you put down the gun now, and we walk out of here together. Let's put an end to this awful night."

"I don't think I can do that, Mr. Conrad. Once I knew you and your partner were on to me, it was just a matter of time and my life as I knew it would come to an end."

"Paying the consequences for our sins actually sets us free, Andy. We can look in the mirror and know with certainty that we paid the full debt to society, just as God paid the full debt for our wrong-doing, no matter how bad it is," reasoned Doug.

"I've seen movies about prison life. I would never survive it, and I refuse to live in fear, having my masculinity stripped from me."

With that comment, Doug saw Andy's plan and knew that things were deteriorating very quickly. Andy had had a plan all along.

"Andy, you have a fiancée and a mother, along with other family members who love you. More trauma could destroy them. Let's end this peaceably."

"I need to ask you one more question, Mr. Conrad, and I need to know the truth. Promise you won't lie?"

"I promise," said Doug, not knowing what the question would be.

"Did my dad include me in his will? I need to know."

Doug hadn't anticipated that question. If he lied to Andy, Andy would know. The last thing the kid needed in his life was to have another person he trusted lie to him. And yet if he told the truth, Andy would realize he killed two people for money he would never have gotten his hands on, so it was all futile. That would make this situation even more precarious.

Andy saw Doug's hesitancy and interpreted it.

"Well, did he?" Andy asked once again, pressing him for an answer.

"I believe *your dad hadn't seen you in nearly ten years Andy. You had rejected him, refusing to make any contact with him whatsoever. He was, as you know, a very philanthropic person . . ."*

"So the answer is 'no.' He gave it all away for good causes."

"I think so."

Before Doug could even react, Andy stood up and pressed the gun into his belly and fired. The explosion was eardrum breaking loud, and Andy dropped to the floor. The apartment door flew open and the police rushed in. Mitch, Donna Gifford, and Barnabus remained at the door in stunned silence.

Doug screamed for the EMS and was on the floor cradling Andy in his arms. Blood was pouring out of Andy's abdomen.

"Help is on the way, Andy. Hold on, son."

"Thanks, Mr. Conrad. You were the only person who would tell me the truth. Tell Wendy . . ." and with that Andy Chandler took his last breath.

Rita heard the shot ring out but realized she was locked in the back of the police car. She didn't know what happened, for she wasn't able to see down the outside corridor to Andy's apartment, but somehow she knew. Her face was pressed against the car window and she was wailing.

Wendy rushed out of her car and ran to Andy's apartment door. Barnabus and Donna Gifford saw her running toward them. Barnabus stepped out to block Wendy and Donna, much to Wendy's surprise, put her arm around her and embraced her.

"You can't go in there, Wendy. I'm so sorry. I'm Detective Donna Gifford, and I'm so sorry. Andy took his own life."

Wendy became hysterical.

"Did Andy really kill his dad and stepmother?"

Donna shook her head in assent. Wendy's leg collapsed and Donna went down to the ground with her.

"I'm so sorry, sweetie. I know how hard it is to lose someone you love. I'm so sorry."

CHAPTER 74

Doug knew the EMS was too late. Andy was gone. He had really thought he could turn the situation into a positive one—that Andy would surrender, but he had already had a decided heart after talking to his mother. Her admission to the lies took away his only justification for the killings. The end no longer justified the means. Andy, then, could no longer accept what he had done.

He wanted to pay for his crime his way. He needed to pay for them. Forgiveness. It's available to everyone and yet used by few. Did Andy ever understand forgiveness? It's not a reward that must be earned.

Sgt. Parker walked over to Doug who was still holding Andy in his arms.

"*At least he didn't die alone,*" said Doug.

"*No, he didn't, Doug. You did the best you could. Let's go.*"

Sgt. Parker escorted Doug out of the apartment where he was met by Mitch and Barnabus. He saw Donna on the ground consoling Wendy. It was a dreadful night with a bad outcome.

Barnabus reached down and assisted Wendy up. The police walked over and asked Wendy to go with them. Donna stood up and hugged Doug.

"*This was a heart-breaking case, Doug, but we did everything we could. Not every case comes out like we want it to.*"

Sgt. Parker walked over to Doug and put his hand on Doug's back.

"It's late, Doug. We'll take the report tomorrow. Go home and try and get some rest."

Doug shook his head in agreement. Barnabus insisted on driving Doug home in his car. Mitch followed behind in Doug's car. Tomorrow would be a new day and a new case, but the tragedy of Andy Chandler would never ever be forgotten.

Made in the USA
Lexington, KY
20 May 2012